THIRD
MAN
OUT

Stonewall Inn Mysteries
Michael Denneny, General Editor

DEATH TAKES THE STAGE
by Donald Ward

SHERLOCK HOLMES AND THE MYSTERIOUS FRIEND OF OSCAR WILDE
by Russell A. Brown

A SIMPLE SUBURBAN MURDER
by Mark Richard Zubro

A BODY TO DYE FOR
by Grant Michaels

WHY ISN'T BECKY TWITCHELL DEAD?
by Mark Richard Zubro

THE ONLY GOOD PRIEST
by Mark Richard Zubro

SORRY NOW?
by Mark Richard Zubro

THIRD MAN OUT
by Richard Stevenson

LOVE YOU TO DEATH
by Grant Michaels

Richard Stevenson

THIRD MAN OUT

A Donald Strachey Mystery

St. Martin's Press   New York

This is a work of fiction. All characters and events portrayed in this book are fictional, and any resemblance to real people or incidents is purely coincidental.

Design by Judith A. Stagnitto

Library of Congress Cataloging-in-Publication Data

Stevenson, Richard.
    Third man out : a Donald Strachey mystery / Richard Stevenson.
        p.   cm. — (Stonewall Inn mysteries)
    ISBN 0-312-08906-6
    I. Title.   II. Series.
    [PS3569.T4567T45   1993]
    813'.54—dc20   92-37743
                                                          CIP

First Paperback Edition: February 1993
10 9 8 7 6 5 4 3 2 1

To Else Harris

THIRD MAN OUT

1

I almost asked John Rutka if somebody had shot him in the foot—I knew plenty of people who'd have loved to—but before I could, he gave me a look of astonishment and said, "I've been shot. One of them actually *shot* me."

"Somebody shot you in the foot?"

"One of them tried to kill him," Eddie Sandifer said, "but they only got him in the foot."

Sandifer looked stunned too, and uncharacteristically shaky; ordinarily it was these two who inspired anger and fright, and Sandifer seemed unsure of what to make of this turn of events.

"It must have been somebody I outed," Rutka said, and looked down, appalled, at the bandaged foot. "God, they're even sicker than I thought. I knew some of them were pathetic, but this is something only a psychopath would do."

We all peered down at the foot as if it might add something on its own behalf. I'd walked over to Albany Med from Crow Street to visit yet another dying friend when I ran into Rutka and Sandifer, and we were in the parking lot outside the E.R., standing in vapors rising from the tarmac after an early evening thunderstorm. Everybody looked purple under the arc lamps, spooky in the urban miasma. Ambulances coasted in and out through the mist, the Tuesday night torn and traumatized delivered as swiftly and silently as Fed-Exed envelopes. Somebody was probably working on a way to fax them in.

Rutka's wound was to his right foot, which he lifted from the pavement a few inches, his right arm over Sandifer's shoulder for support, while he described the incident. As I listened, I tried to concentrate on the narrative and not become distracted by Rutka's wandering left eye, which, in his excitement, was now all over the place.

The loose eye was Rutka's one physical imperfection, the flaw that confirmed the beauty of his sturdy frame and curly-headed Byronic good looks. Watching Rutka was sometimes like looking at a Romantic poet as rendered by a cubist, and you had to be careful not to let the visual spectacle get in the way of Rutka's spiel, which was forceful in its single-minded way but lacked the quirky surprises of his appearance.

Eddie Sandifer listened with eyes half closed to Rutka's recitation, nodding occasionally as Rutka backed up to clarify a point or add a detail; this was probably the third or fourth time in the past three hours that Rutka had told the story of the shooting, and esthetic considerations were already starting to color the reportage.

From time to time, Sandifer reached up to wipe the purple sweat from his face and head; though in his early thirties, like Rutka, Sandifer was nearly bald, his dome glistening. Bathed in the weird light, the stocky, fair-skinned Sandifer looked like a big, masculine, radioactive baby. Both were wearing jeans and yellow-and-black Queer Nation T-shirts, the two of them composing a walking-and-talking embodiment of postmodern gay liberation ideology: We're queer and we're here to stay and you'd damn well better get used to it.

At about four-thirty that afternoon, Rutka said, he had walked out of his house on Elmwood Place, a few miles up the Hudson from Albany in the town of Handbag. He crossed the front porch, started down the front steps, heard a loud crack, and suddenly found himself sprawled on the walkway leading down to the street. His breath was gone and his foot was screaming with pain.

Rutka said he hadn't noticed anyone—Elmwood Place was a dead-end street with just nine houses along it—but he thought he heard a car driving away fast. The car sounded as if it had a defective muffler. When he caught his breath, Rutka shouted Eddie's name several times. No one else responded to Rutka's cries; apparently everyone along the street was sealed off behind closed doors and windows with air conditioners battling the Hudson Valley August heat.

A minute later Sandifer, who'd arrived home from work just moments before, came outside and found Rutka. They had planned on walking down to the Kon-ven-You-Rama store four blocks away to pick up some ice cream sandwiches. Rutka's addiction to sweets was notorious; his dishier gay enemies predicted it was only a matter of years, or months, before Rutka began to exhibit physical defects numbers two and three—bad skin and obesity—and those enemies who were under the impression that Rutka would care one way or another welcomed the prospect. I'd once seen Rutka shrug and say he had more important things to think about than the way he looked.

"Shouldn't you be in a wheelchair or something?" I asked Rutka, who probably wasn't much of a chore for

3

the beefier Sandifer to hold up, but it didn't seem smart to risk stepping on a gunshot wound.

"John is leaving the hospital against medical advice," Sandifer said, with a look of uncertainty. "That's how the resident phrased it. Those guys have to protect themselves, they're so afraid of lawsuits."

"It's not that I don't trust the doctors here to treat a gunshot wound," Rutka said, and hobbled several steps with Sandifer's help to lean heavily against the side of a car, an astonished-looking little Ford. "If American medicine hasn't figured out yet how to treat a gunshot wound, it hasn't learned anything. But I know there are plenty of people at Albany Med who hate my guts, and I'll feel more secure if I can recover at home. It's no big thing anyway—a superficial wound and the ankle bone is chipped."

"John outed one of their board members here a couple of months ago," Sandifer said. "You probably read about it in *Queerscreed*. Certain people were pretty pissed."

As a deeply skeptical—and always faithful—reader of Rutka's tabloid, *Queerscreed*, I remembered. "Merle Glick. What'd he do—vote against extra funding for the AIDS unit or something?"

"He's an absolute sleazoid," Rutka said, nauseated by the man all over again. "Glick is the most famous rest-stop queen from Kingston to Glens Falls, and my source on the Albany Med board says he's the most homophobic scumbag in the hospital."

"Can you believe the flaming hypocrisy?" Sandifer asked. "That man is evil."

"The E.R. staff threw this up to you?" I asked. "They knew who you were?"

"They knew," Rutka said. "When the resident recognized my name, he gave me a look I can only call total revulsion."

This seemed a little off. It was unlikely that the emer-

4

gency-room nurses and medical residents, whose concerns tended to be narrow and immediate, would feel, much less exhibit, indignation over the fate of Merle Glick, a hospital director best known around Albany for enriching his insurance agency with city contracts procured through his connections with the Democratic machine. Though if Rutka said he saw a look of revulsion in his doctor's eyes, maybe he did. It was an effect Rutka often had on people.

"What did you say to the doctor?" I said. "Maybe it wasn't just your name that got a reaction."

Sandifer glanced at Rutka apprehensively, as if my remark might trigger a speech, but it got only a little half smile. "No, he knew me, that's all," Rutka said. "I suppose the Queer Nation shirt might have set something off, too. I know you've got a skeptical mind, Strachey. It's one of the things I've always liked about you, despite your refusal to always back up your words with actions."

This last referred, I guessed, to my failure the previous spring to join ACT-UP in an occupation of the state legislature. An arrest and conviction would likely have resulted in my losing my private investigator's license, my sole means of livelihood—Timothy Callahan having made it plain that if he had wanted to share a mortgage with a man with a criminal record, he'd have picked a crook with a numbered account in Zurich and not a man with a lien on his eight-year-old Mitsubishi.

Nettled by Rutka's ever-superior tone—I was as uncomfortable with his personality as I was doubtful about his tactics—I said, "How do you know you were shot? Was a slug recovered? The actual bullet?" Ruka gave me his gimlet look. "Who's investigating this?" I said. "The Handbag cops? Who did you report it to?"

"What are you trying to insinuate?" Sandifer said, looking as if he might be about to put me in a category.

Rutka just stared at me, and before I could "insinuate"

5

that the two might have staged the shooting for their own strategic purposes—Rutka had stated publicly that in the cause of "gay survival" the end always justified the means—he said calmly, "Yes, a shell was found. The cop didn't find a weapon, and they're still looking for the bullet, I think, but a slug was found by the Handbag cop who answered Eddie's call. The shell was in the gutter about fifty feet from the house, where the car was probably parked with the pig in it who shot me. The cop showed us the slug while I was being put into the ambulance. God, it was hard to believe such a tiny piece of metal was part of what hit me. It felt like getting slammed in the foot with a sledgehammer."

"There was just one shot? That's all you heard?"

"I think so," he said. "It happened so fast, I'm not sure. I guess they'll talk to other people in the neighborhood, won't they? Somebody must have seen something."

"They'll ask around. That's what they do. Even though their opinion of a man in a Queer Nation shirt is probably lower than their opinion of a nun at a school crossing who gets shot, they'll be obliged to make some inquiries."

Sandifer said, "I don't suppose there's any point in expecting the Handbag police to bust their butts going after this guy unless they're pressured into it. We'll probably have to organize something."

"Maybe," I said. "Although small-city police departments can usually be counted on to perk up when they run into an attempted murder. It's a little unusual and it's a challenge. And your chief out there, Bub Bailey, is supposed to be a competent and decent enough guy. That's his reputation."

"My dad knew him," Rutka said gloomily. "They were in the K of C together and bowled when they were younger."

"That should help keep Bub's interest up too. The

6

chief probably regards you as a Martian, but if you're one of the parish Martians he'll feel obliged to nudge the case along."

Rutka looked at me with one eye, and with his other at an ambulance arriving off to the left. He gave a little mirthless laugh and said, "This *is* queer. One of Dad's bowling buddies lending a hand to Queer Nation. It doesn't surprise me, though. Those guys stuck together even if they had a fag son. Dad would have done the same—for somebody else's son."

"He's not living?"

"No, he's dead," Rutka said. "My father died last summer and my mom a month later. They were both fifty-five. They had short lives and unhappy deaths from lung cancer. We all smoked at our house. My sister and I started when we were twelve, and I quit when Dad was diagnosed. Mom didn't give it up until they brought in the oxygen and somebody told her if she lit up she might blow up the neighborhood. It was the only time during the whole ordeal when I ever saw her cry. She wept for her lost Chesterfields."

I hadn't had a cigarette in ten years, but every time I heard one of these horror stories, I ached for one. I said, "That's when you came back to Handbag from New York? When your parents were dying?"

"Eddie and I moved into my old room. They had to have known we were boyfriends. We'd been active in ACT-UP in the city and talked about it. But they always treated Eddie as if he was a school friend I was having sleep over. This is when Eddie was thirty-one and I was thirty."

I said, "What if somebody had written a column in the *Times Union,* or whatever paper your family read, about John Rutka, the homosexual? How would they have reacted? How would you have liked it?"

Without hesitation, Rutka said, "The question is aca-

7

demic. The *T-U* won't out anybody—unless, of course, they're busted by the Albany cops for sex in the park, or some asinine thing like that. Now that I'm a notorious public fag, though, they'll probably write up the shooting as an attack on an 'admitted homosexual.' Since I'm not a convenience store, they won't be able to bury it as just another robbery attempt by a deranged member of Albany's poorly disciplined underclass."

This didn't answer my question or address at all Rutka's apparent double standard on the question of involuntarily dragging gay persons out of the closet into a homophobic glare. But with him leaning awkwardly against a car, supported by one foot and a sweating man with a glistening lavender dome, it didn't seem like the time or place to pursue it.

I asked Sandifer to give me his version of the shooting incident, and he gave me a look of frustrated befuddlement. "I'm just not sure what happened," he said. "The thing is, I was in taking a whizz and I must have flushed just when it happened. I knew I heard something—or thought I did. And then I went out and found John on the front walk. At first I thought he fell down the porch steps—they're getting kind of rickety. And then I saw the blood and John's sneaker torn up. But I don't really know what I heard. I wasn't listening for anything."

Sandifer glanced at Rutka, as if looking for a cue to add more or open up another area of discussion, but Rutka was busy watching me watching Sandifer. I asked Rutka if he had received any physical threats from people he'd outed in his controversial journalistic career during the past year, or from anyone else.

"Too many for me to count," he said with a snort, "and almost all of them anonymous. Nine were from people I could identify. I keep a file."

"You're quite an accountant."

"Not an accountant, a nurse. Nurses spend half their lives doing reports and not leaving anything out and not making mistakes. Keeping records is as natural to me as breathing."

"Were these threats written, or oral, or what?"

"They were all verbal. Who's going to be stupid enough to put a death threat in writing? Two were face to face, in the presence of other people. Seven were on the phone, people calling me, usually late at night, and of those seven, four identified themselves and three didn't but I recognized their voices. I've got notes on all the threats in my files."

Rutka's files. These alone seemed enough to get a person shot in the foot. I had never seen them—no one had, that I knew of—and that only made them all the more tantalizing, and for a lot of people inflammatory.

Since Rutka and Sandifer had moved back to the Albany area a year earlier, Rutka—who'd been active with assorted radical gay groups in New York and had been arrested and fined twice for demonstrations inside St. Patrick's Cathedral—had become Albany's own "morally correct J. Edgar Hoover," as he'd once phrased it to a local TV newswoman.

Rutka had compiled files on hundreds of Hudson Valley "known homosexuals," as he called them. He seemed to love taking this menacing term from the fifties and by throwing it around airily, ironically, defusing it.

Except, for a lot of closeted and semicloseted gays, Rutka might as well have *been* Hoover or McCarthy. He began by using his column in the alternative weekly *Cityscape* to out some of the city's most notoriously, and dangerously, homophobic gay men and Lesbians: an eager aide to a state senator who led the fight to kill an anti-gay-bashing bill; an editorial writer at the sneeringly reactionary Albany *Times Union;* and an antigay Albany

9

city councilman. These revelations, which caused countless dinner-party shouting matches over the ethics of uncloseting any gay person against his or her will, were minor compared to what came next.

Rutka began outing gay men and women who were not necessarily wicked and dangerous, but merely prominent: several business owners; a local TV weatherman; pols of all stations and creeds; the inevitable slew of Episcopalian clergy; a miscellany of others.

Since there is nothing wrong with being gay, and since heterosexuals' dating and mating habits were described all the time, well-known people had to expect this, Rutka said. His column, called "The Society Pages," was Rutka's way of helping "normalize" being gay and removing its stigma for future generations.

When, on right-to-privacy grounds, *Cityscape* finally rejected Rutka's arguments and dropped his column, he began putting out his own tabloid, *Queerscreed,* which was printed at the Kopy-King franchise where Sandifer was assistant manager and then passed out on the streets by Albany's tiny Queer Nation membership. Rutka's column became even nastier in tone and closer to out-and-out hysteria in *Queerscreed*—"You are worse than AIDS, worse than gay-bashing, you KILL US WITH YOUR HYPOCRISY!" he often screamed in print at his subjects. This disturbed Albany's more sedate gay pols and organizers who'd made gains in recent years using more conventional means, and who feared a backlash.

But Rutka was undeterred. He continued to build his files, and to make enemies. One of whom apparently had now tried to rid closeted gay Albany forever of what a middle-aged, previously closeted gay mortuary owner had recently called "this McCarthy in sheep's clothing."

When I asked Rutka if he planned on turning over his files to the Handbag police for use in their investigation, he said gravely, "You can't be serious," and looked at me in amazement, as if *I* were the one going around opening up gay people's lives to the scrutiny of the public and the state.

"John, if there's been an attempt on your life," I said mildly, "it's only logical that an important part of any intelligent police investigation will be the questioning of people who felt threatened by your campaign. You said yourself that that's who you thought took a shot at you, somebody you'd outed. Or were planning to out, you might have added."

"No," Rutka said, with a little shake of his head, "I really think *I* have to be the judge of what use my files are put to. If the cops ever got hold of my unpublished material, who knows *what* they might do to people."

This was said with not the least trace of irony. And although I could see that Rutka had a point, if somebody had insisted to me that within twenty-four hours it was going to become my point too, obsession even, I'd have said I didn't think so.

2

Up in a fifth-floor corridor, outside Stuart Mese-role's room, I met Timmy and told him about the shooting incident and my encounter with John Rutka.

He said, "Too bad Rutka wasn't bending over kissing his own foot when the shot was fired. He might have died in a characteristic pose that would have pleased those few who would cherish his memory, and the rest of us would be rid of him."

It was indicative of the effect Rutka often had on people that his misfortune could produce so harsh a response in so rational a soul. Normally a purveyor of Franciscan charity and the very soul of Jesuit restraint, Timmy had often spoken critically of Rutka, especially since Rutka's outing of a friend of Timmy's, a state legislator from one of the Southern Tier counties whose voting record on gay matters was impeccable but who had chosen to remain closeted out of deference to the sensitivities of his father, an Orthodox rabbi. The old cleric had performed his own monumental act of paternal love by refraining from hurling lightning bolts at his fallen son, the *feygele,* and merely spent his evenings weeping.

12

"Nobody deserves to be shot," I said. "Gunshot wounds are always worse than they look even in the movies these days, and they hurt a lot."

"Good."

"And if Rutka had been shot dead," I said, "you wouldn't have liked it. You would have hated it."

"Not him."

"When you told Eldon that Nicky Mertz died, and Eldon said he didn't want to hear about it—'What's one more?'—you almost punched him, you were so mad. You revere life. You're an authentic papist."

"St. Augustine," he said. "Fourth century. Killing another human being can be justified to combat a threatening evil."

"He meant war. The Roman Empire was about to be attacked and the previously pacifistic Augustinians worked out a theory of a just war that would lead to a just peace. They didn't advocate popping off people who were mere pains in the ass."

He looked at me oddly. "How do you know all that?"

"You explained it to me fourteen or fifteen years ago. It was soon after we met. It might have been within the first five or ten minutes."

"You're right. It's starting to come back to me."

"How is he?" I said.

"There's no change. He's the same as he was yesterday, and the same as he was the day before, and the same as he was the day before that."

"Is Mike in there?" I could see the bed nearest the door with its comatose occupant, but not beyond the curtain to the room's second bed, where Stu Meserole lay, also in a "persistent vegetative state," sustained through tubes by machinery that bleeped and ticked dully, not convincing as a life force.

"They're all in there behind the drape. Mike and Rhoda and Al."

"Do they leave after Mike leaves, or are they afraid he might sneak back?"

"No one knows. Rhoda and Al appear to live on another plane of existence from the rest of us that precludes such mundane matters as coming and going. It is beyond our knowing."

"Nah, we could find out."

"I don't think so."

"Rhoda and Al," as Stu Meserole had always referred to his parents, whom he feared and adored despite their coldness toward Stu's lover and friend of twelve years, Mike Sciola, had dedicated their every waking moment to keeping their son breathing even after his brain had been largely eaten away by a ferocious cancer previously found only in kangaroos.

Stu, like Mike, had been found to be HIV-positive six years earlier. Each had defied the odds by remaining entirely healthy until the previous May. That's when Stu had a headache one day, was blind a month later, lost most bodily functions soon after that, screamed and talked gibberish for a week, then went to sleep. The cancer then inexplicably quit growing and left Stu with just a few critical functions, including respiration.

Mike wanted to find a way to let his friend, whose mind and soul were gone, go all the way. Rhoda and Al Meserole didn't. They believed in science and they believed in miracles. They believed one or the other would bring their son back to tortured wakefulness. Stu, having neglected before he suddenly fell ill to complete the proper New York State forms designating Mike as his "health care proxy" and the decider of his fate, was now legally under the control of Rhoda and Al, who feared that Mike would "pull the plug," as they put it, an actual

14

plug indeed being down there somewhere to tug out of a wall socket.

Mike wouldn't have pulled it—he had other means in mind, it soon developed—but the Meseroles knew their man, and he knew they knew him. The three of them spent many hours each day in Stu's room eyeing each other whenever they weren't flipping through *TV Guide*, or staring at the soaps, or gazing out the window at the June blossoms and then the ripening summer.

Timmy and I dropped by several evenings each week to try to lure Mike away. He didn't have to go to work until close to Labor Day—to his job as a high school social-studies teacher out in Balston Lake—but he was losing weight and his friends feared that his self-neglect would trigger an opportunistic infection and he would fall apart, too. We and a few other friends had become regular standees outside room F-5912, at the end of a corridor not in the AIDS section of the hospital but in a chronic-care unit where Stu and his immediate neighbors were all, as we'd heard one intern put it, "turnip city."

Stu shared a room with a skeletal, vacant-eyed Hispanic man no one had ever been known to visit. Across the hall lay a truck driver rendered comatose when his semi overturned on the Thruway. Sharing the trucker's room, in an uncharacteristically democratic gesture—and possibly as a cost-saving measure for the not-so-flush-as-it-once was Albany diocese—was Bishop Mortimer McFee, who'd slipped on a lovingly waxed rectory floor in mid-June and landed on the back of his head, and now lay in medical and presumably spiritual limbo somewhere between the Albany diocese and the seraphim.

Traffic in and out of the bishop's room was considerable. Priests, mayors, nuns, columnists, restaurateurs, a U.S. senator, the lieutenant governor all came and went with whispers—apparently so as not to disturb anybody's irreversible coma—and heads bowed. One day Timmy himself had even looked in on the bishop to offer a mild novena for the soul of this man who had once told a Catholic gay group they would not be allowed to meet in a church's sub-basement because it wasn't "low enough for the likes of you."

"I went in and forgave him," Timmy told me when he came out.

"And did a look of peace spread slowly across his visage?" I asked.

"You're being sarcastic," Timmy replied, and said no more. On certain topics I never was sure what was going on in his head and knew enough not to try to find out.

Mike Sciola wandered out of the room now, dazed and bleary-eyed, and radiating the heavy medicinal scent carried by people who spend hours a day in hospitals. His cheeks were gaunt under his graying beard, and his dark hair was matted with sweat.

"Thanks for coming," Mike said.

"No change?" I asked.

"Nah."

"How are Rhoda and Al?"

"The same."

"Can you talk to them at all?"

"Not about turning off the feeder. If I talk about who's on Oprah today, they're cordial enough. But if I try to talk about Stu, forget it."

"You might as well quit for the day," Timmy said. "Visiting hours are nearly over anyway. Have you eaten?"

"I ate something."

"I haven't eaten at all," I said. "Let's walk over to Lark Street and sink our teeth into something greasy and refreshing."

"I guess. Maybe in a while."

16

"Somebody shot John Rutka," Timmy said. "Did you hear?"

This got a rise. "Holy shit, is he dead?"

"I just talked to him down in the parking lot. Whoever it was just clipped him on the foot and he's not too bad off."

Sciola's red eyes were alert now. "I'm amazed it didn't happen sooner. You can do what that guy's been doing in New York or Hollywood and get away with it, I guess, but Albany's too straight and nineteenth-century. Gay people just aren't used to that radical stuff around here. I've seen guys who are ordinarily levelheaded go absolutely bananas when the subject of John Rutka comes up. I've even heard people say somebody should shut him up permanently, and some people seemed to mean it."

"Who did you hear say that?" I said.

He had to think about this. "Well, Ronnie Linkletter. I heard him say one time Rutka should be boiled in oil. Maybe that sounds as if he was speaking figuratively, but he said he'd love to light the match. And when the other people who were there joked about a John Rutka fondue party with Rutka the thing being fondued, Ronnie said he wasn't kidding, that anybody who set out to ruin people's lives had to be stopped, and if the legal system couldn't do it then it was all right for people to do it on their own. He really seemed serious."

"Was this before or after Ronnie was outed?" I asked.

"Well, I think it was actually before, believe it or not."

"Ronnie must have known he was an easy target," Timmy said, "being a media superstar and all."

"He's still there doing the weather on Channel Eight, isn't he?" Sciola asked. "I can't stand to watch those shows."

Timmy said, "They make *USA Today* look like *Le Monde.*"

I said, "They're trying to push Ronnie out. They've got him on at some godawful hour in the morning, instead of at six and eleven, but he's got a contract. I've heard he's looking around though, in places like Yuma and Winnemucca. He's been hurt and I'm sure he's very, very angry at Rutka. Who else have you heard say anything threatening?"

Sciola mentioned three other people: a closeted Albany cop he knew; a Schenectady dentist whom Rutka, to my knowledge, had not gotten around to outing; and a married Lesbian vice president of an Albany-based bank. Their remarks, as Sciola recalled them, were vaguer than Ronnie Linkletter's, and less menacing. They were not, in fact, much different from comments I'd been hearing directed at Rutka at gatherings for the past six months. I told Sciola this and said I could probably compile a list of twenty-five people who'd been pretty nearly unhinged by Rutka's crusade and had shown it in public.

"So half the gay people in Albany are logical suspects," Timmy said. "Maybe they all did it. It's like *Murder on the Orient Express.* Everybody had a motive and everybody had a hand in doing it."

"In shooting a man in the foot?"

"That would explain why they only got him in the foot. It sounds like an assassination attempt by a publicly appointed commission."

Sciola managed a wan smile and said, "I'm tired. Let's get out of here and eat something. Someplace with cold beer."

"I'm for that," Timmy said.

"Let me just check on Stu," Sciola said, looking suddenly apprehensive. He turned and strode back into room F-5912. Ten minutes later, when he hadn't come out, I waited while Timmy went downstairs to find a vending machine. He came back with two Snickers bars and a foam cup of watery coffee.

18

"He hasn't come out yet?"

"He says we should go ahead. He's not hungry."

We left the candy bars and the coffee on the floor outside the room and went out into the semitropical Albany night. We weren't so hungry ourselves anymore and rode over to the house on Crow Street in Timmy's car.

The eleven o'clock news on Channel Eight led with "an attempt on the life tonight of a controversial gay activist in a residential neighborhood in Handbag." Rutka, who must have phoned the TV stations just after I left him in the hospital parking lot, was seen on his front steps grimacing and condemning homophobic murderers.

The report was brief and the interview heavily edited. It did include Rutka's comments that "internalized homophobia" was gay people's biggest problem and that from then on "no gay hypocrite in Albany will be safe" from Rutka. A spokesman for the Handbag Police Department said only that the incident was being investigated.

3

Rutka phoned the first thing next morning. "I need your help," he said.

"I don't think so."

"It's the Keystone Kops out here—the Keystone Kops on Quāāludes. They're useless."

"It's too early to tell."

"No, it can't be too early, it can only be too late. If they don't catch whoever shot me and arrest him, he could try it again. Or somebody else who'd like to get rid of me might see how vulnerable I am and come after me. I have to know somebody's working on this who knows what he's doing if I want to feel secure enough to go on with my work."

On with his work—Albert Schweitzer at Lambaréné. I said, "I'm not sure how I feel about your work. No, that's wrong. I disapprove of a lot of it. When you crossed the line from the Roy Cohn types to the merely well-known, you lost me. That's not fair."

Timmy looked up from his Cream of Wheat and mouthed, "Rutka?" I nodded. He looked down again.

20

"No, it's fair," Rutka said. "Until this heterosexist society knows that we are everywhere, that a high percentage of the most popular and respected people from every area of American life are gay, gay people who are ordinary can never begin to be accepted and feel safe. It's the moral responsibility of every gay man and woman to act as a role model and to . . ."

He gave me his stump speech. I listened and watched Timmy trying to read my reaction across the cereal. I consumed most of three eggs, up, and an English muffin while Rutka orated.

When he wound down, I said, "I'm pretty much with you on the social analysis but not on the tactics. Doing unto ourselves as others would do unto us can't be the answer. Anyway, whether I agree with you or not is academic. The shooting is a police matter and you should give them a chance and see what they come up with. Maybe they'll surprise you."

"Are you tied up with anything else?"

"As a matter of cold, hard fact, at the moment I am at liberty. But that's beside the point. Also, I do this for a living. I cost money."

"Not always. I've heard about that. But that doesn't matter. I can pay you. I have income from the hardware store. Dad left the business to me and Ann. She runs it and draws a salary, but we split the profits. I have a decent income. What do you charge?"

Timmy was seated behind a container of the clotted sweet tea he had become addicted to in his Peace Corps days in India back at the end of the Pat Boone era, and as he sipped the roily substance, he watched me with growing apprehension.

I said, "I wear red suspenders, drive a week-old BMW, and charge ten thousand dollars a day." Timmy gave a little nod of approval.

21

Rutka said, "Seriously."

"Seriously, my pants are held up by a disintegrating belt I picked up at an after-Christmas sale at Penney's in 1974, I drive an old Mitsubishi with rust spots on the doors, and my rate is two hundred dollars a day plus expenses."

"That's reasonable. I'd like to hire you."

"To do what?"

"To find out who shot me and have him arrested."

"I'm telling you, John, that's the Handbag Police Department's job. That's how they'll see it and they'll be right. Police departments solve crimes."

"They can't do it."

"You don't know that," I said. "You insist on fairness but you're not being fair."

"I've never insisted on fairness. If you believe that, you don't understand me at all. It's too late for fairness. I want change. I want people to confront their own bigotry, and I want this society to confront its own ignorance and stupidity, and I want bigotry and stupidity to wither under the harsh glare of the sunlight of truth."

"Oh, well. I stand corrected."

A silence, then a long sigh. "Look, Strachey, just put yourself in my place, will you do that? Think how you'd feel and how you'd react if somebody shot a gun at you. Have you ever been shot? I'll bet you have."

"No, just at. They missed."

"But still, you know. You were very frightened."

"Yes."

"And you wanted the person who did it caught and locked up immediately."

"I sure did."

"Then you can begin to understand what I'm going through. How would you feel if your life depended on the level of competence at the Handbag Police Department?"

22

He had me there. "I guess I'd feel the way you do. Endangered."

"Whatever you think of me, should I be shot and killed?"

"I'm one of those who don't think so, no."

"And what about those who *do* think so? Can the Handbag Police Department protect me from them?"

"Maybe." When I said "maybe," Timmy's look of apprehension deepened.

"When it's your life, the only one you'll ever have, 'maybe' isn't good enough. Am I right about this?"

"Sure." I looked away from Timmy, out the kitchen window at the box of pink petunias Timmy's Aunt Moira had hauled up from Poughkeepsie on the front seat of her Dodge. The thunderstorm the night before had bent them low, but in the morning sunshine they were starting to perk up nicely. With my well-practiced peripheral vision I could make out Timmy's mouth hanging open lightly. If I'd put a square of glass in front of it, I'd have gotten a little moisture.

"Don't you sometimes do security work?" Rutka said. "Protect people and property for a fee?"

I said I'd done it from time to time.

"Well, how about protecting me? The fact is—" There was a tremulous pause. "The fact of the matter is, Strachey, I'm scared to death. I really am. This time I really put my foot in it. I went after somebody who must be totally wacko. Whoever it is wants me dead and there isn't a fucking thing I can do about it. I'm vulnerable and I don't know what to do. For God's sake, can't you help me just because I'm fucking scared and I want help? I'll *pay* you, for God's sake, but I really *need help.*"

He waited. "I could talk to you," I finally said to the petunias.

"Will you?"

"It would be a security thing."

23

"That's what I mean."

"Did you ask the police for protection?"

A half-laugh, half-sob. "They're going to drive by the house once an hour. A fucking lot of good that will do as soon as the killer sees them leave for the next fifty-nine minutes. Or if I leave the house to go anywhere."

"This is true. You're not as well protected as you might be."

"Bub Bailey said they were short-staffed, it being August and vacation time for some of the officers."

"I couldn't stay with you twenty-four hours a day," I said. "If you wanted bodyguards I'd have to hire them and that could become expensive. Is that what you think you want?"

"I'll have to think about that."

"But I could spend some time with you, become a known presence that would have the effect of unbalancing somebody trying to get at you. And I could advise you on precautions to take."

"That could help a lot. And while you were around, I could fill you in on the people who would be the most likely to try to get at me. And naturally you could go through my research material and maybe come up with some leads on your own—stuff you could pass on to the cops without them having to go directly into the material, which I am not about to let the government see."

I said, "Oh, your files, right." I looked Timmy directly in the eye and tried not to blink.

"You might spot something I missed myself," Rutka said. "I've got tons of notes and letters and memos. Sometimes I can't even read the handwriting. Mine or somebody else's."

"I could sift through it. It couldn't hurt. And if I ended up assisting the police in their inquiries in a small way, maybe they would appreciate it, if I was tactful."

24

"I can't tell you how relieved I am," Rutka said. "You might think I'm dogmatic and overly aggressive, but I'm human too and you recognize that. Whatever some people think I have coming, I don't deserve to be shot dead."

"No."

"Can you come out here this morning and we'll talk? I'm supposed to stay off this foot."

We set a time and he gave me the address.

As I hung up, Timmy set down his mug. "Why are you doing this?"

"Several reasons. Two, anyway. Three."

"This guy has done things that turned your stomach."

"He's also done things I approved of. Bruno Slinger, for one, had it coming." This was the state senatorial aide who had lobbied vigorously, and successfully, to have a hate-crimes bill killed. I said, "Having that low slug sautéed was a public service worthy of a Nobel Prize."

"The Nobel Prize in outing?"

"Biophysics, then."

"Except the stunt backfired, because Slinger is a man comfortable with the big lie. He just denied it and said the fags were trying to smear him. What good did any of it do?"

"It did some good," I said. "People believed it. They don't take Slinger as seriously anymore. His effectiveness could be cut down. People snicker at him behind his back."

"Indeed they do," Timmy said, looking both smug and disgusted, one of his more practiced expressions. "But they don't laugh at him because he's a liar and hypocrite and probably borderline psychotic. They do it because he's gay. He's another wretched homo. See, that's my point: When Rutka outs the monsters, people start talking about monstrous homosexuals. When he outs nice guys who are just well-known, then people talk about gay people as pathetic victims. Either way distorts the truth and hurts the cause. Rutka is unfair and he's wrong and he's dangerous."

I said, "I know. I mean, I agree with you up to a point."

"Which point?"

"Irrationality has its uses. Irrational people have theirs. They draw attention to a problem that's pretty much ignored otherwise, and then the more rational people on the same side of the issue move to the forefront and get taken seriously and the problem starts to get solved." Then I added, all too superfluously, "Sometimes you have to crack a few eggs to make an omelette."

"Oh. Oh, please."

I hardly believed I had uttered anything so callously puerile to Callahan, no matter how offhand. I knew that it would not have passed muster at Georgetown, to which Timmy returned every five years along with other alumni to have the gilt on his high moral tone freshly applied, and I doubted the argument would even get by at Rutgers anymore. But I played out my assigned role in our customary dialectic nonetheless, and said, "Progress is necessarily messy. Simply getting straight America's casual acceptance of gay people requires a lengthy battle in which collateral damage is inevitable. Some people are going to get hurt. But it's necessary and it'll all be seen to have been worth it in the end."

He made a little explosion of air that sounded like "Splooooph." He said, "I thought you were in favor of the all-volunteer army. And I know you're against cruelly mindless euphemisms."

"Yes, I am against conscription," I said, "unless people are routinely offered a choice to do something nonmilitary that will contribute to the common weal. And I'm not even so sure about that."

"Right, you're not so sure. Because you believe that in

a civilized society people should pay taxes—even plenty of taxes—to buy civility and to help out the unlucky, but otherwise people who obey just laws should be pretty much left alone. I've heard you say that."

"Yup. Pretty much."

"So if the government of a nation that calls itself civilized should let people alone, *why shouldn't John Rutka let people alone?*" He raised his voice, a rare occurrence.

I'd had enough. "Well, on second thought, maybe you're right. As usual."

He snorted and began gathering up the soiled china and utensils. "Donald, I cherish you." He snorted again and turned on the hot-water tap all the way, as his mother had taught him, to prepare for scalding the dishes and cleansing them of the *Trichomonas,* cholera, scurvy, and athlete's foot that surely were lurking there. He said, "So it sounds as if you're going to go to work for this man you disagree with and don't like. Why?"

"I've worked for lots of people I disagreed with and didn't like. If I hadn't, I'd've starved."

"But this is a special situation. And I know you don't need the money. What you made from the Hapgoods should carry you well into the fall." This was a recent case wherein I discreetly recovered a purloined family portrait—the grandmother of a Presbyterian grande dame from Latham in a pose startling even by present-day standards and barely imaginable in 1878, the year of its creation—and received for my efforts an appropriately obscene fee.

"No, I don't need the money," I said. "Though Rutka claims he can afford it and he's paying me."

The scalding process began; you could almost hear the little screams of the rinderpest. "Then why are you doing it?" he said.

"Three reasons. One, I don't need the money now, but

27

I might need it later. This is a chancy business. The second reason is, Rutka is in danger and he's frightened. He needs protection—not from criticism or maybe even from the odd sock in the jaw. But he does not deserve to be shot and killed."

"That's two reasons. What's the third?"

I knew he'd guess. "It's the least important of the three."

"Uh-huh."

"You don't know?"

The faucet was shut off, the cloud of steam began to dissipate, and he looked at me. "You want to get a look at his files."

"I'm curious. I admit it."

He began to laugh. "People deserve their privacy. Except you'd like to get just one little peek."

"Something like that."

"I know what you mean. Naturally I recognize the impulse."

"Except you would never act on it, would you?"

He thought about this. "I can't say never. I'm not perfect."

"Yes, but your imperfections lie in other areas."

This was irrelevant and unfair and I wasn't sure why I said it. He knew exactly what it meant, and briefly he was struck uncharacteristically speechless.

Timmy's imperfections had been a sensitive topic in recent months. The previous spring he had had a terrified hour-and-forty-five-minute sexual assignation with a diminutive huge-eyed Bengali economist who was passing through town. It had been Timmy's first lapse from his fourteen-year pledge of sexual fidelity. (I had made no such promise, and we had survived the onset of the HIV plague by the skin of my teeth.) Though health precautions were taken, he *had* done it, he immediately confessed, when he'd become unhinged, he said, by the little professor's uncanny resemblance to the district poultry officer Timmy had had the unrequited hots for in Visakhapatnam in 1968.

It may have been the briefest midlife-crisis fling on record, and it was only minimally hurtful to me—except to the extent that the incident was so out of character I feared that Timmy might be coming down with Alzheimer's, rare as it is among men in their forties. The event passed quickly by and was rarely referred to anymore, except on those occasions when I would get to point out that even a man educated by Jesuits could make a mistake. "Yes, every fourteen years," was the usual reply to this.

This time he was late for work, he said, and didn't have time for a nervous jocular exchange at his expense. He trotted upstairs to finish getting into his legislative aide's duds. With an hour to kill before I headed out to Rutka's house in Handbag, I read the newspaper account of Rutka's run-in with "an assailant possibly angered by exposure of his homosexuality." When Timmy sped through, I kissed him, careful not to leave egg on his lip.

4

The first thing Rutka said was, "I want to write you a check for the retainer. Will two thousand be enough?"

"We can work that out. Five hundred should do for now. Tell me about your visit from the Handbag police."

It was mid-morning, cloudless and heating up fast, and we were seated on the screened-in back porch of the old Rutka home on Elmwood Place, a short street of angular frame single-family homes separated by narrow lawns and driveways leading to small garages at the rear of each property. The elms of the street name apparently had succumbed to blight, but young maples lent some shade to the well-kept houses, whose cozy front porches were fortified by puffy hydrangea bushes and bosomy heaps of respectable shrubs. It felt like an unlikely locale for a Queer Nation headquarters, but maybe that was the point.

Each house had a concrete walk leading down to the street, like a tasteful necktie. Some were lined with zinnias and marigolds in lurid full bloom. The flowers lent a note of welcome to the neighborhood, though as I'd driven up no human being was visible. Up the street a gray cat had scratched a hole in a garbage bag left at curbside and was rummaging through the spillage. The only sound was from a dozen or so air conditioners scarfing up what was left of the Mideastern oil reserves in atonal tandem.

Rutka, pale but otherwise shapely and fit in cut-offs and a tank top, was sprawled along an old metal fifties-era porch glider on a bed of cushions that looked as if they'd been dragged down from the attic every summer since the glider was purchased. His wounded appendage lolled over the side of the glider below a sinewy leg and well-turned, muscular thigh that was not the result of a health-club regimen, I guessed, but of a decade of plowing up and down hospital corridors eight to twelve hours a day.

I sat in a metal rocker and helped myself from time to time to an M&M from a large dish on an end table next to Rutka. He ate them by the fistful, as if the medical advice he'd received had been to stay off the wounded foot and eat plenty of candy. My peripheral vision searched his torso for love handles but none were visible. I chewed and swallowed my own M&M's slowly so as to distribute their effects evenly.

"The stupid cops thought what I thought they would think," Rutka said. "That I shot myself, or Eddie shot me, for the publicity and the martyrdom. God, I'm mad but I'm not crazy."

"They said that straight out?"

"They didn't have to. They asked me if either Eddie or I owned a firearm, and they kept asking me to repeat the story of what happened, over and over, as if they couldn't quite believe it, or they were trying to trip me up."

"Did they trip you up?"

"Look, I know what happened. No, they did not trip me up." Rutka's left eye wandered off to take in the old grape arbor, heavy with bird-pecked pale produce, that extended down the backyard away from the porch, and his right eye peered at me beadily. "I went outside, somebody shot me, and a car drove away. How could anybody trip me up? Even if I was making it up, it's too simple."

"Tell me again everything that happened from beginning to end. Start when Eddie came home from work. Is he at work now?"

"He works every day, including Saturday, from seven-thirty to four, later when they get busy. Yesterday was slow and Eddie was home by four-thirty." He repeated the story he had told me the night before in the Albany Med parking lot: Eddie's arrival home; the plan to walk down to Konven-You-Rama; stepping off the front steps; bang; car with bad muffler speeds off; Eddie comes out, finds Rutka sprawled; cops, ambulance arrive; shell found in gutter by patrolman.

Rutka's story sounded identical to the narrative I'd heard the night before. A new detail cropped up here and there; others were dropped. It sounded real, natural, truthful.

"You said the cops asked if you own a firearm. Do you?"

"I told them I didn't. But I do. I guess I can tell you."

"Oh, great."

"Here," he said, and slid a .38 Smith and Wesson revolver out from under the cushions.

I examined the weapon, which was fully loaded, and said, "Where did this thing come from?"

He was nonchalant. "Around the corner from my old apartment on a Hundred and Sixth Street in New York.

32

I bought it retail, I guess you could say. These things are easier to come by in that neighborhood than take-out Szechuan."

"It's not registered anywhere?"

A mirthless laugh. " 'Register criminals, not firearms,' right, Strachey? How could I be a First Amendment purist and scoff at the Second?"

"You're right. Criminals should be required to register their crimes in advance and observe a seven-day waiting period before committing them." I returned the revolver and Rutka stuffed it back under the cushions. "How come you felt you needed one of these?" I asked.

"In New York," he said, "I was mugged twice by gangs of kids. After the second time, when they threw me in the gutter and hit me on the neck with a chain, I bought this gun from a guy I knew at the local bodega. Of course, it didn't do me any good. It was too much trouble to drag it around and I always left it at home. You can't hide a shoulder holster under a nurse's uniform."

"What was the caliber of the slug the cops found yesterday?"

He shrugged. "They didn't tell me. But it wouldn't have come from this gun. That I know."

"Because?"

"Because this gun was up on a closet shelf in our room. I brought it down this morning when Eddie left for work. I didn't really know how scared I was until Eddie left and I was alone. I have to admit, I really started to freak. That's when I called you. And I got the gun out and loaded it."

Rutka was looking directly at me now with both eyes, though if a wild man suddenly arrived on the scene spraying hot lead it wasn't at all certain where an excited Rutka's gaze might land. I said, "You have one eye that wanders. If you had to shoot that gun, how would you aim it?"

"With my right eye," he said. "It's the left one that gets away. That'd be no problem."

"Makes sense. What about the actual bullet that nicked your ankle? Have they found it yet?"

He took another fistful of candies, chomped on them, and said, "Two bozos were out here with tape measures and geometry-class instruments at six this morning, but they didn't find anything. They said they thought the bullet might have buried itself in the lawn. I got the impression that if I'd been shot through the pancreas they'd've dug up the lawn. But they said there was no reason to make a mess in the neighborhood if they didn't have to. They went through the motions."

I asked him for the names of the investigating officers and he said, "Just the chief—Bub Bailey—and the patrolman who was here last night, Octavio Reed. They only have one detective in Handbag, and he's on vacation until Labor Day."

The name Octavio Reed meant something to me, but I couldn't remember exactly what. I said, "They told you that?"

"They were civil," Rutka said with what looked like a trace of disappointment. "The chief mentioned Dad, of course. It was obvious he wasn't going to tell me what he really thought of me in the presence of Dad's ghost. The reactionaries who control this country are right in one way—what they call family values *are* worth something. Just make sure you're a member of the family. And that you don't have one of those families that, when they find out you're queer, they kick you out on the street."

"I take it that wasn't the case with you."

His face tightened and he said, "No. I was lucky in that respect. Actually, they didn't know. I was pretty fucked up as a kid. I kept everything hidden. My first experi-

34

ences were not what you would call ideal. I didn't really come to terms with my sexuality until I was in nursing school in 1980 and met some gay people who had their shit together. And even then I didn't come out and start thinking of myself as gay until I hit New York.

"I got down there just in time for the plague, which was horrible, but fortunately I met Eddie a couple of months after I arrived. He was just out of the Marine Corps and really ready to let loose too. We hardly got out of bed the first month we knew each other, we had so much sex and emotion pent up inside us. I brought him home whenever I came up, and everybody in my family just sort of knew. Ann said they figured it out when I decided to become a nurse. How's that for sexual-orientation stereotyping?"

"Competent enough."

"So they knew, and it seemed to be okay, just as long as nobody spoke the dreaded word."

"And you never spoke it?"

"Nah. Not in Handbag. Not until later, in New York, when I went to a couple of ACT-UP meetings and started to understand how all-pervasive homophobia is in this society and how it kills people. Then I spoke the word."

"I suppose," I said, "Chief Bailey was forced to speak it when he was here, or at least to allude to it."

Rutka sneered. "He said he thought the shooting might have had something to do with my being 'an activist.' That's all he said, 'an activist.' "

"And you conceded there might be a connection?"

"He asked me for the names of anyone who had threatened me in recent months, and I gave him my list."

"You have a little list."

"These are the ones who I know who they are. I've gotten so many anonymous threats in the past year I've lost count."

He reached over the edge of the glider, retrieved from

35

the end table a photocopied single sheet of paper, and passed it to me. As I read over it, Rutka scooped up another handful of M&M's and crunched on them noisily while I studied his list of names and brief biographical descriptions. The list had on it the state senate aide, the TV weatherman, and seven other names I recognized from Rutka's *Cityscape* outing column and from *Queerscreed*.

I folded and pocketed the list and said, "These are all people you've already outed. You haven't been threatened by anybody who hadn't been outed yet but was afraid you might go after them? Somebody in your files?"

"No. Not yet."

"Where do you keep these famous files, anyway?"

"Hidden."

"Here in the house?"

"Upstairs. I'll show you. They're locked up. Eddie has a key. I have a key. And I'll show you where there's another one. Nobody else has ever seen the files."

"I'm flattered."

"You should be. I take my responsibilities with the data that I've gathered very, very seriously."

This was an interpretation of Rutka's activities that would have been challenged through clenched teeth by many in Albany, but I was now his security consultant and not his conscience, or linguist, and I let it go.

"How did you compile these files?" I said. "How do you dig up all this dirt on people?"

"I'm surprised to hear you call it dirt," he said, looking annoyed. "That's a retrograde term I'd expect to hear from a person who has internalized his or her own homophobia."

"That's what I meant. It's dirt to them."

"Exactly. So, Strachey. You're a detective. If you were going to build up a set of files on homophobic closeted people, how would you go about it?"

"I'd keep my eyes open and ask a lot of questions wherever gay people congregated. I'd stake out cruising areas and see who turned up. I'd make myself available to people who wanted to sell information that somebody somewhere would consider damaging. And of course I'd cultivate in-the-know gay people who share my beliefs about outing or who might be brought around to my way of thinking."

He nodded. "You've got it."

"I'd build up a network of informants, too. In the police department, among the press, maybe in the area's hotels and motels, where lots of gay people are employed, and closeted gay people show up for trysts wearing shades and red wigs that don't fool sharp-eyed nosy desk clerks and room-service waiters and busboys."

Another nod.

I said, "I guess the motives of your informants don't count for much. Just so they deliver the goods."

He looked at me with both eyes and said gravely, "I occupy the high moral ground in this. It doesn't matter if many of my informants don't. They can deal with their own consciences. I'll deal with mine. I think of tips from sleazy people as just that—tips, leads. I would never out anybody on the say-so of just one person, even if that person was sincere and reliable—which some of them are. They aren't all scuzzbags.

"That's why it pisses me off that people say I use McCarthyite tactics. Joe McCarthy was reckless and sloppy. He'd go after somebody on the basis of anonymous calls or letters from crackpot organizations. I would never do anything like that. The idea of it makes me sick."

When I thought about it later, Rutka's indignantly drawn fine distinction between his approach and Joe McCarthy's kept blurring in my mind. But as Rutka sat there on a sunny Wednesday morning shaking his head

37

in disgust over McCarthy's failure to double-check his sources, he came across as the consummate professional: exacting, judicious, fair-minded, wise: the Benjamin Cardozo of outing.

I said, "Well, John, whatever I might think about your outing campaign and the way you go about it, you've convinced me that I can rely on your skills as a researcher-reporter. That's quite a data bank you must have stored away up there. And I guess I agree it's all but certain that the name of the person who shot you is buried somewhere inside those files. So if I'm going to help keep you from getting shot again, we should get to it. It's time for me to take a look at those files."

Rutka seemed to pause for just an instant to consider the gravity of the step he was about to take, and then he swung both feet onto the floor, sat up, and reached for my hand.

5

Rutka slid up the stairs backwards on his seat, pushing himself upward with the good foot. On the second floor he pulled himself upright and hobbled into a dim bedroom with drawn shades that had been a teen-aged girl's in the early seventies and had been frozen in time: orange shag throw rug; pink chenille bedspread with a heap of stuffed animals on the pillows; a stack of Carole King records; an Osmond Brothers poster on the wall; some group photos showing the Handbag High cheerleaders hoisting their pom-poms and thrusting up their breasts with military precision.

"Your sister's room?"

"You are good."

Rutka unzipped the belly of a stuffed hippopotamus and pulled out a set of three keys. "Now you know where a set of keys is, in case I'm not here."

Down the hall, he unlocked the attic door with two of the keys and we climbed up, him on his seat. The wall of dry heat that hit us when we got to the top felt like a visit to Khartoum. I helped support Rutka and we bent low so as not to have our skulls pierced by roofing nails. Past the piles of old furniture and boxes labeled "xmas" and "grandma," at what I took to be the rear of the attic if my orientation was correct, was an old World War II–vintage desk.

A light bulb on a wire dangled overhead. Heaps of old *Cityscapes* and *Queerscreeds* were on the floor off to one side, and on the other stood a two-drawer metal filing cabinet. The heat was awful under the uninsulated shingled roof, and Rutka switched on a box floor fan that just blew the hot air around; I tried to remember the Arab word for the madness caused by this type of wind.

Rutka used a third key on his chain to unlock the file cabinet. Down below a phone began to ring, but Rutka gestured to never mind. "The machine will pick it up." He perched on the edge of the desk and said, "This is it. The famous files."

I slid open the top drawer. It was jam-packed with file folders arranged alphabetically by outee.

"The ones with the red tags have already been done," he said.

"I'd have expected an up-to-date guy like you, John, to be computerized."

"My financial resources are not unlimited, despite what I'm paying you. I'll stay here while you look through them. You'll probably have some questions."

We were both sweating now from the heat. The main effect of the fan was to dry the sweat on our body surfaces and blow occasional droplets onto the stack of files I spread out on the desk. My neck itched and we both stank. Rutka seated himself on an old kitchen chair next to the desk and made notes in the margins of a file he retrieved from a desktop box labeled "current" while I spread out the *A*'s.

"What's that?" Rutka said, listening.

40

I heard it too, the sound of glass breaking, a bottle or jar smashing.

We listened.

"I'll check," I said.

Before I even made it to the stairwell, a smoke alarm down below began to wail. I hurtled down to the second floor, and even faster to the first, where dark smoke was boiling into the kitchen. Out on the back porch, flames, fed by what smelled like gasoline, were roaring up from the floor. The glider cushions were ablaze, and even the M&M's, drenched by the blazing fluid, were melting and popping in the billowing fire and smoke.

I grabbed the canister fire extinguisher by the kitchen door, yanked the release handle, and directed the hose at the conflagration. White foam shot out with enough force to make me bobble the awkward tube, but I regained my aim and sprayed the glider and floor repeatedly with the retardant chemical. The flames vanished in spots, only to spring up again when I shifted my aim. Hacking and gasping and weeping from the smoke, I doused the area with chemical until the fire was extinguished. I found a phone in the kitchen, dialed 911, and asked for the Handbag Fire Department to come out and make sure the fire was out. Then I examined the damage.

Rutka, having made his way down from the attic, appeared in the hallway leading to the kitchen and peered at me with a look of horror.

"Oh, Jesus, what happened? What blew up? Oh, God, now what!"

"I hate to tell you."

"What? What happened?"

"There's a hole in the back porch screen, and there's broken glass on the porch floor. It looks as if it was done deliberately with a Molotov cocktail."

He fell against the doorsill. "Oh, God. I did it. Now I really did it!"

"It looks that way."

The smoke alarms were still wailing and I got up on a chair to disengage the one in the kitchen. I was about to head upstairs to shut off the alarm there when sirens sounded out on the street. I thought of something and sped back out to the porch and snatched up Rutka's hot revolver with a towel and handed them both to him to hide. He flung them into the oven and slammed the door shut as I went on up to disengage the second-floor alarm. When I came back, a police cruiser was parked outside, lights flashing, and Rutka was opening the front door for a Handbag patrolman who looked dimly familiar. He caught my glance and blinked. Then a fire engine roared up in a manner that might have successfully intimidated a small blaze into extinction. As the rescuers barged in, Rutka directed them to the rear of the house.

To me, Rutka said, "Maybe you'd better lock the attic door."

He passed me the keys and I moved up the stairs quickly. I secured the attic and was headed back down when I caught a glimpse of myself in the mirror at the end of the hall. My face was sooty and my hair was a tropical rainforest. I dashed into the not-so-fastidiously-kept bathroom and washed the grime off my face as well as I could, drying off with one of the rancid towels heaped on the floor by the shower. I dumped the stale water from a grimy glass on a shelf by the sink and gulped tapwater from it, salve for my dehydrated throat and insides.

Back downstairs, the firefighters had declared the blaze extinguished, but for safety's sake they were wetting down the smoky and charred area of the porch with a fluid from their own canister. Rutka was speaking with the fireman in charge and explaining what had happened.

"That's what it looks like to me," the fireman said disgustedly. "I'm going out to call the fire marshal right now. Don't touch anything out there. They'll need to check the place out for what they can find."

"I won't touch it."

"You can air the place out—set up some fans. Nobody saw it happen?"

"We were upstairs," Rutka said. "We heard the bang and my friend here ran down and put the fire out. I've got a wounded foot."

The fireman looked down and shook his head. "You were lucky. You were just darn lucky somebody was here."

Rutka looked at his foot and said, "I know."

"You ought to call your insurance man," the fireman said. "The damage should be covered."

The Handbag police patrolman who had come flying up Elmwood Place just ahead of the fire engine had been entering and exiting the house busily throughout the activities of the past fifteen minutes, and now he returned and was listening intently to our conversation. "OCTAVIO T. REED," read the nametag on his uniform. He had slicked-back dark hair, and liquid brown eyes in a broad face that was bunched up now in a kind of quizzical squint. His shoulders were slumped forward almost disconsolately, it seemed. I remembered now where I knew him from: we'd met at the Watering Hole and spent half a night together at my Morton Avenue apartment in 1975 or '76, after which, I thought I recalled, he said he had to get back to his recent bride in Handbag.

While the fireman went on talking to Rutka about insurance and cleanup matters, Reed beckoned and I followed him outside.

"Long time no see," I said.

He glanced around nervously. "I don't go out any-more. I've got kids in school and I'm a police officer and—you know."

"How long has it been?"

"It was July of nineteen seventy-six," he said. "You're one of the ones I like to remember."

"It's pretty clear to me, too. I don't go out anymore either. I've got a boyfriend. I met him not long after I met you."

He looked at me wistfully. "All that time."

"Are you still married?"

"Sure."

"Is it a good marriage? I mean otherwise."

"Yeah," he said. "That's the trouble."

The firemen were coming out now and starting to pack up their pumper. Reed looked around and said, "Are you still a P.I.? I've seen your name in the paper."

"I am."

His look darkened. "You're not working for this Rutka, are you?"

"As of today, I am. On account of what happened last night—the shooting. He hired me."

"Maybe I shouldn't be telling you this, but I hate to see you get involved with this guy. I was just out going around the neighborhood trying to turn up anybody who saw anything at the time the fire started, and I got one. There's an old lady over on Maplewood Place whose bathroom window looks out on Rutka's backyard here. She says she saw somebody go through the backyard and up behind Rutka's garage before the alarm sounded and the fire department got here. She says it was Eddie Sandifer."

"She saw him herself? She's sure it was Sandifer?"

"That's what she says."

44

"Interesting."

"Be careful of those two."

"I've been being careful of them, but maybe not careful enough."

6

Reed got into his cruiser and rode away, and I went back into the house and looked up the Kopy-King number. I checked my watch—11:57 A.M., about half an hour since the fire started—and dialed. Sandifer answered.

"Hi, Eddie, this is Don Strachey. Do you know what's happened out here? I'm at the house in Handbag."

"What happened? What do you mean?"

"There's been a fire. It's okay, it was put out without much damage, but somebody threw a firebomb onto the back porch. It looks like another attack on John and it was sort of a close call."

I could hear his breathing quicken. "Is John all right?"

"For now. Later I'll try to get him to a safer place."

"I've got my lunch break," Sandifer said. "I'm coming out. Don't leave till I get there, okay?"

"How long does it take to drive out here?" I said.

"Twenty minutes. I'm leaving right now."

"See you soon."

Rutka was seated at the big mahogany table in the dining room looking morose and going through some

46

papers he'd taken out of a drawer in the sideboard. "I guess I'd better call the insurance agency. Even though those people are such a hassle."

I said, "I phoned Eddie. He's driving out."

"I know. I heard you."

"He's concerned about you, he says."

He continued to peruse the documents. "If he wants to come out, fine. Though you're here now." He looked up. "You're not crapping out on me, are you? Now that I'm relying on you more than ever?"

I looked at him but didn't answer.

"I don't have any friends in this town," he said.

"You do have enemies. That I believe."

Now he looked worried. "Is there something you *don't* believe?"

I seated myself in the chair across from Rutka and looked into his face and said, "The cop who was here asked around the neighborhood for people who might have seen something at the time of the fire. He found one."

Rutka blinked. "He did?"

"A woman on Maplewood Place was looking out her bathroom window, which overlooks your backyard."

"Vera Renfrew."

"She told the cop she saw someone she recognized cut through her back yard and into yours before the fire started. Guess who she says she saw?"

"I don't know. I'd love to know. Who?"

"Eddie. She saw Eddie Sandifer."

He slumped forward and shook his tresses. "Oh, no."

"Can you explain that, John?"

He kept shaking his head. "She told this to that dumb cop?" He was grinning stupidly.

"That's what I've been told. The police will pass it on to the arson investigation unit."

Rutka suddenly went all red and he glared at me

fiercely. "I'm being set up," he said. "I'm being goddamn fucking set up." His left eye headed west.

"By Eddie?"

"No, no!" he snarled, his dark locks trembling. "Of course not by Eddie! I'm being set up by Bruno Slinger, that sleazoid scumbag! Slinger and Grey Koontz are trying to frame me."

"Who," I said tightly, "is Grey Koontz?" My head had been feeling hot and greasy on the outside and now it was starting to feel hot and greasy on the inside, too.

"Koontz is one of Slinger's tricks and a dirtbag from the word go. He looks a lot like Eddie, except maybe younger, maybe twenty-four or -five. From a distance, or even in a dark bar or someplace, people sometimes get them mixed up. Slinger must have planned the whole thing after I outed him. He's one of the ones who threatened me and he is absolutely ruthless, ask anybody. It was probably Koontz or Slinger who shot me last night, and now they're trying to frame Eddie, the fucking degenerates!"

I looked into the one of Rutka's eyes that was looking at me and said, as calmly as I could, "Are you using me?"

"No. Not underhandedly, if that's what you suspect."

"Don't. I'll catch on. And then you'll have another enemy."

"I wouldn't. I know you're sharp, Strachey. That's why I hired you. If I wanted to run a con on somebody, I'd do it with those stupid Handbag cops. Trust me."

I said, "The Handbag cops aren't doing badly at all, so far. And it strains credulity way past the limit that the famous senatorial aide you outed should have a boyfriend who looks just like your boyfriend and would be in a position to frame you. That's quite a coincidence."

"They're not boyfriends," Rutka said, and turned to snatch a Snickers bar from the sideboard behind him.

"Koontz is an occasional trick, that's all. It's in the files—you'll see it. Slinger's current boyfriend is Ronnie Linkletter. I can't imagine that wimp Linkletter coming after me. But Slinger and Koontz—those two douche-bags are capable of anything."

He went to work on the candy bar and I sat there watching him eat. "Are you hungry?" he said. "Help yourself."

"No."

He finished the sweet. "You don't believe me, do you?" he said, giving me his poor-misunderstood-thing look.

I said, "It's about the dumbest explanation I ever heard."

"No, it's not," he said, looking bitter now. "It's the obvious explanation. Just because you've never seen Grey Koontz, you don't believe it. What kind of solipsis-tic bullshit is that? If you have no personal knowledge of something, then it can't be true? I thought you were smarter than that. What other explanation could there be, anyway? Eddie was at work. He was there when you called."

"I called half an hour after the fire started. It takes twenty minutes from here to Kopy-King. Eddie could have been back with plenty of time to spare."

He waved this away. "All right, he could have done a lot of things, but he didn't. Look, the cops will check Eddie out, and where he was at the time of the fire, and then you'll be satisfied. In the meantime, who knows what that fucking Slinger has in store for me next. If you want to be skeptical, be skeptical. I don't care. Spend as much time investigating Eddie as investigating me. Just help protect me, will you? If you want to think of it as protecting me from myself, go ahead and think of it that way. I'm going to write you a check right now." He pulled out a checkbook from under the stack of documents.

I said nothing and watched him write the check, and I thought about it. Then I made a decision. More out of curiosity over what I had come to see as a fascinating disturbed personality with a tiny role to play in gay history—more for that than for any other reason (such as my wanting to get a longer, closer look at the despicable files), I said, "John, I'm willing to work for you for the next twenty-four hours."

He said, "That's a start."

"I'm not going to cash the check," I said. "And if at the end of twenty-four hours I have concluded that you have lied to me and involved me in an elaborate hoax, I'll return the check personally and I'll stomp on your shot foot. How's that?"

He handed me the check. "I understand your position," he said. "You have a reputation to protect and you have to do what you have to do. But I'm not worried. I don't have much to fall back on, but I do have my personal integrity. And if that's your only concern, I'm on firm ground. Just let me know when your belief in me has been restored."

Restored? I said, "Do you want to stay at my place overnight? You'll be safe there, I'm certain."

"That's not really necessary. Eddie will be here and we can take turns sleeping. I think my gun was damaged in the fire, but Eddie has another one."

"Registered?"

"No. From the bodega, like mine."

"I'll try to get the Handbag cops to increase their coverage of the house. After the fire, that should be no problem."

He agreed and I phoned the Handbag police station. I reached Octavio Reed, who said, "Before we do anything at all out there, you should talk to the chief. He knows of you and he wants to meet you. Don't say anything about—you know."

"No way."

"Chief Bailey wants to see you this afternoon if you can make it. He's out right now. Can you come at two?"

"I'll be there."

"Just don't trust those two," he said, and rang off.

"I'm meeting the chief this afternoon about arranging additional protection," I told Rutka, and could see him working up to a fit over the delay, when Sandifer walked in.

"Oh, jeez, look at the porch! This is— Oh, jeez!"

"It's a mess," Rutka said.

"Are you okay?"

"Yeah, but there's a ridiculous new development that I should tell you about."

"What?"

"Vera Renfrew told the police she saw somebody suspicious go down her yard and up ours before the bomb was thrown."

Sandifer stared. "She did?"

"She said she saw you."

Sandifer's face fell forward, along with much of the rest of his upper body. "Oh, that's just great," he said finally. "Jeez, why would she say a thing like that? That's crazy."

"I guess it was somebody who looked like you," Rutka said.

After a brief, frozen instant, Sandifer said, "Oh, no, not—"

"It makes sense, doesn't it?"

"Grey Koontz."

They went on in this vein for some minutes, and I kept thinking, They had a scam worked out that went awry and now they're making it up as they go along.

51

7

The insurance agent soon showed up, trying to look delighted about shelling out a few thousand of the home office's zillions, and while he and Sandifer and Rutka surveyed the reeking and charred mess on the back porch, I went upstairs.

En route to the attic I looked into Rutka's and Sandifer's room and spotted the telephone answering machine Rutka had mentioned earlier. The message light was blinking. This had to have been the call Rutka and I had heard from the attic a few minutes before the fire broke out, and which Rutka had said not to bother with.

I pushed the playback button. There were a couple of clicks and that was it. The caller had hung up.

In the attic the sauna heat hit me again. It was hard to imagine that men paid large sums of money to join fashionable clubs so that they could sit around in places like this and perspire recreationally. I peeled off my sopping polo shirt and hung it over the front of the whirring box fan.

The file I pulled out first, on Bruno Slinger, was thicker

than most. It contained press clippings on the Republican state senator Slinger worked for, and Slinger, as the senator's occasional spokesman, was quoted from time to time, always in support of conservative causes: anti-abortion, anti–social services, and, amazingly, antigay. News photos of the senator in groups often included Bruno Slinger in the background.

Slinger had an easy, smug look in his press clips, but in his other photos he was more somber. In one Polaroid his cheek was bulging with the erect member of a physically fit Caucasian male whose bare upper body was out of the shot. The member was condomless, not a good idea anymore. The notation on the back said "Slinger and G. Koontz" and gave a date from the previous fall.

Handwritten notes by Rutka paired Slinger's name with those of a dozen or so other men, with dates and locations noted, most of them motels in the Albany area. The name Grey Koontz did crop up several times. I reexamined the photo with "G. Koontz" on the back to see if the man in it resembled Sandifer, and while their builds were similar, the focus on the man's organ rather than his face made evaluation difficult. Still, it occurred to me that Rutka and Sandifer might actually be telling the truth about a Slinger-Koontz frame-up attempt.

Several handwritten letters were in the Slinger file, each in a different script. One, dated the previous October, began: "Hi, John. Just thought you'd like to know that Bruno Slinger is a cocksucker." It was signed "A. Friend." There was no return address; the mailing envelope stapled to the letter was postmarked Albany.

Another note read: "Bruno Slinger is gay. Check it out." No signature or return address on that one either. A third, also unsigned and from Albany, informed the reader that "Bruno Slinger goes for boys." This could have meant underage youths or boys of thirty-five; the

53

rest of the letter described in unoriginal language Slinger's sexual practices and gave no further clue to his age preferences.

There were several similar letters offering firsthand knowledge of Bruno Slinger's homosexuality, and there were fifteen or twenty letters—often typewritten and literate—lacking evidence of personal experience but insisting on the fact of Slinger's queerness just the same. Many of these ill-wishers were especially venomous and used words such as "twisted" and "monstrous" and "evil" to describe Slinger's hypocrisy.

The Slinger file also included a note in Rutka's handwriting describing an anonymous phone threat, which Rutka speculated had come from Slinger. The caller had said, "You're going to get your balls ripped off for this one," and the call had come just a day after Slinger's outing in *Cityscape*.

I flipped back to the file for Ronnie Linkletter, the Channel Eight weatherman Rutka said Slinger was now involved with. Linkletter's file was a thick one too. It contained a multicolor promotional brochure put out by Channel Eight detailing the weatherman's part in the station's "We're Hometown Folks" campaign. This was where the station's news "personalities" went out into the community and showed, a tad superfluously, that the news broadcast by Channel Eight's newscasters existed in a context not of history but of themselves. They looked happy about this, and according to the ratings, the station's viewers seemed satisfied too. Ronnie Linkletter's part in the "We're Hometown Folks" effort was to go into clubs and schools and relate odd facts of meteorology.

Linkletter also was as comfortable in front of a Polaroid as he was on the Channel Eight news set. Ronnie was belly down in his single blurry snapshot, butt raised for the insertion of a sizeable organ whose owner's face was above the frame.

Linkletter, too, had been tattled on by anonymous letter writers. One began: "Dear Mr. Rutka—I have been reading your column and agree with you one thousand percent that queer people have to rise up or die. A life of oppression is no life at all. . . ." The writer went on to proclaim his philosophical fraternalism with Rutka and then offered the name of a "media celebrity who has not accepted his own queerness but should be made to do so because he is well-liked in the community and would further establish queer omnipresence in the public mentality." The name was Linkletter's and the writer asserted that he once spent a night with Linkletter in the Fountain of Eden Motel on Route 5.

There were other, similar letters—Linkletter attracted a more casual, less incensed type of snitch than Bruno Slinger did—and an assortment of dated notes in Rutka's handwriting describing phone calls about Linkletter. One sheet of paper labeled "From JG—Linkletter at motel with A" consisted of a long list of forty or fifty dates, each of them a week apart.

Linkletter's file also included an issue of the February third *Cityscape* in which Linkletter was outed, and a memo to the file on a phone call from Linkletter to Rutka after the outing, in which Rutka described Linkletter's rage and his stated intention to "bash your brains in." Rough language for a Hometown Folk.

I got out the list Rutka had given me with the names of the other people he claimed had threatened him. Besides Slinger's and Linkletter's, seven threats had been received. The two face-to-face encounters had been with the *Times Union* editorial writer, who met Rutka at Queequeg's restaurant and screamed, "You oughta have your black heart ripped out!"—no Pulitzer material in that—and with a Colonie auto-parts-store manager, who ran into Rutka in Macy's just before Christmas and told him he wouldn't be alive six months from then. Rutka had outlived that prediction already by more than a month.

The other five threats by identifiable people all came by phone. All threatened violent acts, even death; they were from a Schenectady orthodontist, an Albany court bailiff, an elementary-school principal in Troy, a state university physicist, and a retired professional hockey player.

I went through the files and took copious notes on all nine of the men who had threatened John Rutka—for what it was worth. The attacks on Rutka could as easily have been made by one of the "countless," as he'd put it, anonymous callers who'd threatened him. Or by someone who had never threatened him at all. There was always that.

I flipped through a sampling of the other files. Some of the names I recognized from Rutka's columns in *Cityscape* and *Queerscreed*. Others, unouted as yet, were men and women I knew. My stomach began to churn, partly from hunger and partly from disgust, and my impulse was to alert these people immediately that they were on Rutka's list of possible outees. The ethical ramifications of my position with Rutka were becoming more complex by the minute.

That complexity was not lessened when I flipped through the front of the file one last time in search of a name that might mean something to me. I came to another one I recognized and gawked at for some seconds. Here was a file labeled "CALLAHAN, TIMOTHY."

The little bio note attached to Timothy Callahan's folder described him as an Albany man in his forties who worked as the chief legislative aide to New York Assemblyman Myron Lipschutz, and who resided in a house on Crow Street with his lover of fourteen years, private investigator Donald Strachey. The only piece of paper in the folder was a single phone memo dated April 25th: "Parmalee Plaza Hotel informant IDs Callahan entering room with guest who informant says he had the night before."

Poor Timmy. Just once he had embraced in terror the ghost of the district poultry officer he had lain dreaming about uselessly long ago in Visakhapatnam, and in doing so had exorcised that ghost, and now he had his name on an overbearing twit's hit list in an attic in Handbag. This was not fair. My opinion of John Rutka, which had seemed to bottom out in recent hours, began again to slide.

I stuffed my notes in my pocket, put my still-damp shirt back on, switched off the fan and the lights, and returned to the second floor, careful to double-lock the attic door. I zipped the keys back inside the hippo's belly.

With the insurance agent on the way down the front walk toward his burgundy Lincoln, I said to Rutka in the front hall, "My boyfriend's in your file."

A little dry laugh. "I thought you'd get a charge out of that." Sandifer stood at the end of the hall grinning nervously.

"I don't."

"Oh, what the— It's just a fucking file!" He hobbled into the living room too fast, nearly stumbled, and went down hard on the couch. "There's nothing in the file except that one fucking call. What was I gonna do with it, anyway? I can't out somebody who's already out, can I? You two are the most famous queer couple in Albany. In the paper they refer to you as 'the Albany private investigator and acknowledged homosexual,' and Callahan is almost as notorious as you are. So please don't go all self-righteous on me, Strachey, because I would find that very, very hard to take."

57

I said, "What if I hadn't known?"

He rolled his eyes and sighed grandly. "Well, of course you'd know. Or if you didn't know, you wouldn't care. Hey, I know all about you, Strachey. You've been playing around on the side since day one, and it was only reasonable for me to assume that you and Callahan had an open relationship, and he was doing it too, and it was cool. Why are you making such a big fucking thing about this? I don't get it. I just don't get it."

He looked genuinely mystified. Sandifer came down the hall now and stood listening.

I said, "First of all, it's been years since I've had sex with men other than Timothy Callahan. For reasons of avoiding the plague, for Timmy's emotional well-being, and because it just doesn't seem to matter to me as much as it once did, I don't do it. And the fact is, he never did it. Emotionally it is not his style. But whatever the two of us do or don't do sexually, together or with others, John, the simple fact of the matter is, none of it is any of your goddamn business!"

I yelled the last part, and Rutka flinched.

Sandifer went and sat beside Rutka on the couch and took his hand and held it. Rutka's eyes were off in different directions; he began to shake his head from side to side. "Now I'm really fucked. I've alienated you, and I am totally, totally fucked. Oh, shit. Shit, shit, shit."

I'd had enough. I said, "I think I need to get away from you, John. Before I punch your face in." Would I now have to add myself to the list of people who had threatened Rutka? "I'm going over to talk to the Handbag police about getting you some protection. I do believe, John, that you make people want to kill you, and maybe somebody really is trying to do it. You should stay here because the arson squad will be here soon. Eddie, can you wait here until I get back?"

"I'll call in at work," he said. "I can finish up some things this evening."

"Are you going to ditch me?" Rutka said, giving me the evil eye. "Because I left your boyfriend's folder in the file? I could have taken it out, you know. I thought about that. I left it in because I thought the only way you'd work with me was if I was straightforward with you and didn't hold anything back or hide anything. I guess I should have been more devious."

"Removing Timmy's file would not have been deviousness," I said. "That would be called tact—not giving offense when to do so would be petty or needless. But the real problem for me is, John, that there shouldn't have been a file on Timmy up there in the first place, and there shouldn't be a file up there on ninety-eight percent of those people. Just as if I'd wandered into J. Edgar Hoover's personal cache in 1965, your files make me want to throw up."

He got a panicky look. "Are you quitting? Are you abandoning me?"

"Not yet. But I'm close to it. A lot will depend on what I find out about you from the Handbag police."

"Your mind is closed," he said with a moan, and I left.

8

As I pulled out, the arson squad drove up, two guys in jackets in a state car. I left Elmwood Place and turned north out of residential Handbag and past the old brick lady's-pocketbook factories the town had taken its name from in the 1880s. Handbag's last handbag had been produced in July of 1968, when the stitchers and clampers struck for a dollar-and-a-quarter-an-hour raise over three years, and management didn't even schedule a bargaining session. A union leader claimed the managers just left the screen doors flapping and drove out to the airport. I've read there's now a town in Malaysia called Hahndoo-Bahgoo.

The factories I passed were boarded up, some with roofs fallen in. Now people worked down in Albany for the state or in so-called "service industries," some of which were doing something socially useful—fixing cars, deciphering tax forms, delivering pizza—and many of which were not. Employing fifty or sixty people in Handbag was a new outfit I'd read about called Sell-You-Ler Telephone, a telemarketing firm. The company was paid large sums by other companies to bother people at home. It seemed an unlikely way to try to restore American economic competitiveness in the world, but that's probably not what Sell-You-Ler's owners had in mind. As I rolled up Broad Street, there the damn place was. I thought about going in and bothering somebody, but figured they would have systems in place to prevent this.

I grabbed a quick burger at a drive-up window, and when they asked me if I'd like an apple pie for dessert, I asked them if they'd like to read my copy of *One Hundred Years of Solitude,* by Gabriel García Marquez. I said it was a wonderful novel.

The Handbag police station was in a wing of Town Hall, a two-story pale-brick and concrete-slab structure. Bland and easy to take, the building looked like a Jimmy Carter public works project. A clerk behind the counter had never heard of me, but she ushered me to a windowless room with a collapsible table and some folding chairs and asked me to take a seat. I started to count the pores in the beige cinderblock walls, and ten minutes later, at two-fifteen, the door opened and a man shambled in and shut the door behind him.

Chief of Police Harold "Bub" Bailey nodded, shook my hand cordially, and said, "Don't get up." In his gray sports jacket, yellow polo shirt, and khakis, Bailey looked less like a police chief than the manager of a bowling alley, except less harried. Sixtyish, with receding gray hair and a round face with a droll, noncommittal look, he came across as a man alert to his surroundings but not ready to get too excited by them. He seated himself across the table from me and spread out some folders.

"You're a private investigator," he said. "That's the way to live. Take the ones you want to work on and let the rest go. I wish I could get away with that."

"It has its advantages," I said. "Though the pension plan is poor."

"That's something to think about, you bet."

"If you could pick and choose your cases," I said, "would you have picked the one we're here to talk about?"

"I sure would've. Charlie Rutka was a friend of mine and he wouldn't have wanted anything to happen to his son. And I don't want anything to happen to young John, either. That's what I want to talk to you about."

"Good. That's what I wanted to talk to you about."

He fiddled with the folders on the table thoughtfully and said, "How well do you know your client, Mr. Strachey?"

"I've known him casually for a year. This is our first close contact. Why?"

He looked at me somberly and said, "I think that you're a professional and I've heard that you're an honest man."

"I try to be both, but I have lapses."

"I know you've been a gay activist yourself and had run-ins with the Albany Police Department too."

"Sometimes."

"Don't quote me, but you were probably in the right. I know for a fact there are officers in that department whose conduct is not professional."

"That's putting it mildly."

"No," he said, "that's not putting it mildly at all. Those are strong words for me, and when I say a police officer is unprofessional, that's an indictment. It doesn't happen in Handbag, I'll tell you that."

"It's the minimum people should expect from their police."

He said, "I think you also consider yourself a professional, Mr. Strachey, even though the ethics of your profession are probably a little looser than the ethics of mine."

"Probably."

"But not so loose that you could afford to participate in a conspiracy that involved arson and a false report of attempted murder." He watched me and waited.

"Chief," I said, "if you have evidence that John Rutka is involved in such a conspiracy—if that's what you're suggesting—why are you telling me? Go arrest the son of a bitch."

He arched his back, stretching to get a kink out of it, grimaced mildly, and said, "I'll explain that in a minute. First I want to convince you that I've conducted a professional investigation. Are you interested in the evidence?"

"Sure."

"Item number one," Bailey said, "is that a witness can locate Edward Sandifer in the Rutka backyard at the time the fire began."

"There may be a kind of goofy explanation for that."

"Item number two in the evidence file is the fact that Sandifer left Kopy-King half an hour before the fire started and didn't get back to the shop in Albany until twenty minutes after the fire began. The Kopy-King manager says Sandifer was out making a delivery to a customer and he named the customer. We checked that out and it was true. Except the customer, Bernie's Caterers, is just a five-minute drive away from Kopy-King. That's ten minutes round-trip. Where was Sandifer the other forty minutes?"

The question was asked rhetorically, but I went through the motions. "He could have been anywhere," I said. "Picking up a cup of coffee, standing in line at the bank, goofing off. Where did the Kopy-King manager think he was?"

"No idea. He was stumped too. And Bernie's says Sandifer dropped off the order and left immediately."

"Look, Chief, I have to tell you something. I know about your witness on Maplewood, Mrs. Renfrew."

"Good. You're as sharp as I heard you were. So, what'd Edward have to say? What's his explanation for going up the yard just when the fire broke out?"

I looked Bailey hard in the eye and said, "He says it must have been a guy who looks like him—somebody he knows who looks just like him, he says."

"That's not very good."

"There's a guy in Albany by the name of Grey Koontz who's a friend of a man John outed. I take it you've followed John's unusual career in journalism."

"Yes, I have." He tapped another of the files in front of him, a file on the file man.

"Well, this Grey Koontz is supposed to be a pretty low character, according to John and Eddie, and they think Bruno Slinger, a guy John outed, put Koontz up to starting the fire. Slinger got all unhinged when he was uncloseted, and he threatened John. It looks to me as if this Koontz character is somebody you might want to check out."

Bailey sat there slowly shaking his head. "Do you believe a word John Rutka says?"

I wanted to say no, not a single word, including "and" and "the," but instead I said, "He often makes a kind of sense. On the subject of the cruelties and injustices inflicted on gay people in this country, he can be very clearheaded."

"That may be, but it's not what I mean. I mean, does he lie or tell the truth about things that happened or what people said?"

I said, "I'm still sorting that out."

"John Rutka is a habitual liar," Bailey said with a look

64

of melancholy. "He broke his mother's and father's hearts with his lies. From his thirteenth year on, Charlie Rutka once told me, the boy lied about everything from his homework, to his household chores, to where he went when he left the house. He even stole things and lied about that. When he was an altar boy at St. Michael's, he stole a valuable chalice, and when his mom found the chalice in the attic, John blamed his sister Ann. It seemed the boy just couldn't help telling whoppers. He lied all the time then, and I'll give you odds, Mr. Strachey, that John Rutka is still telling lies today. It's too bad, but people who are like that don't often change."

I said, "It discourages me to hear that."

"Of course it does. And here's some more discouraging information." He opened a folder. "In February of last year John Rutka was arrested in New York City for theft of drugs and medical instruments from the hospital where he worked. The charges were dropped when he agreed to resign his nursing position. Fifteen or sixteen other arrests over the past three years are for vandalism, trespassing, and resisting arrest. There were two convictions for trespassing that cost John two hundred dollars in fines each time. Mr. Strachey, I'll bet my bottom dollar you weren't familiar with your client's criminal record, were you?"

This was murky. " 'Criminal record' is putting it strongly," I said. "The trespassing charges were probably ACT-UP zaps—demonstrations against institutions that some people think hurt and kill people with their policies on AIDS and figurative and literal gay-bashing. I haven't done it myself—I don't want to lose my license—but I greatly admire a lot of what they do. As for the drug charge, I'd want to know more about that. It's out of character—he's an M&M addict—and there might be an explanation. You said you had your reasons for laying all this out for me. Let's get to the point. What are you after from me?"

"I want to convince you," he said, "that John Rutka and Edward Sandifer are going to end up in jail if they stay in the Albany area, and I want you to talk them into leaving."

"Oh."

"John apparently trusts you. He doesn't trust me—thinks I'm one of the old farts who hates gays. That's not true. My education and training have taught me to be broad-minded, whatever my upbringing. But John would never listen to me, anyway. He's the family rebel and I'm too much like family. So I want to convince you that John should go out to San Francisco or someplace like that where his type of gays are more welcome and can feel at home. Just pack up and go. Now."

"He'd never do it."

"You can convince him. It's for his own good."

"Chief, I have no idea why John Rutka stayed on in Handbag after his parents died, but he's here and he thinks of it as home, and it's his right to stay here, that's for sure."

"Yes, it is. And it is not only my right but my obligation to prosecute him for any crimes he's committed—provided he's here in Handbag for the prosecution to take place. If he's gone from Handbag for good, I can probably get away with letting a few things slide by. But if he stays, I'll have to charge him, and I'd hate to, really. A lot of people who knew Charlie and Doris Rutka would hate to see it too, including my wife, who was Doris's best friend. See my problem? I don't want to prosecute John, but I will if he stays in Handbag. I'll expose the scam he's working—the arson squad's report will come to me for disposition—and I'll see that he's punished for it. I'll have no choice. Now do you see the situation we've got to deal with here?"

He gazed at me placidly.

I said, "Yes, I think I see what the situation is we've got to deal with. But I don't think John and Eddie are going to see it the same way."

"I'm going to leave that up to you," he said, and picked up his folders.

9

I drove back into Albany, took a ten-minute cold shower, and phoned Rutka.

"I've been threatened again," he said before I could get a word in. " 'This time you're going to burn,' was what the guy said. I didn't recognize the voice, but the asshole scared the shit out of me. Whether it was somebody capable of actually hurting me or not, I don't know, but the voice was full of hatred and I don't want to take any chances. What kind of protection did you get Bailey to agree on?"

The throbbing in the back of my skull that Rutka induced much of the time started up. I said, "That was all the caller said, 'This time you're going to burn'?"

"He said it twice, the same thing."

"To you or to Eddie?"

"To me. I answered the phone. Eddie has the gun and he's watching out the back door and I'm watching out the front. The arson investigators were here, but then they left and we were here alone. We explained to the investigators about Grey Koontz, how that's who Mrs. Renfrew must have seen, and they said they'd check it out. They were businesslike enough. Not exactly friendly, but what can you expect? And then about ten minutes ago this call came in. So am I about to get some protection, or not?"

"I had a long talk with Bub Bailey," I said. "He says he has your best interests at heart, and I think he means it."

A pause. "What is that supposed to mean?"

I recited the whole story: Bailey's evidence eliminating Sandifer's alibi for the time of the firebomb attack, on top of Mrs. Renfrew's placing Sandifer in the neighborhood; Bailey's litany of Rutka's crimes and misdemeanors in New York, as well as his long history of lying; Bailey's offer of a deal—get out of town and don't come back, so that Bailey won't have to prosecute the son of an old friend, as well as the son's boyfriend. I left out the part where Bailey suggested San Francisco as a city where Rutka and Sandifer might feel more at home; mentioning it would only set Rutka off on a tirade whose object was beside the point.

Rutka, of course, came up with his own semi-irrelevancy. After I finished, there was a long silence. Then he said, "Do you have any idea why I took the hypodermic and the drugs from the hospital? Do you?"

"No. Okay, tell me."

"And do you know what the drug was?"

"No. And I don't feel like guessing."

"It was morphine," he said. "Morphine for a man in horrible pain whose body was half gone and who for twenty-four hours a day for a solid week had been begging to die. Do you have any idea? Have you ever been around such horror?"

"Yes, I have."

"Then you must understand. It's not that I shouldn't have taken the drug—nobody will ever convince me of that. It's just that I shouldn't have gotten caught."

"Okay."

69

"Or I should have gotten the stuff on the underground market. That's a lot easier now than it was then, but it was possible and I should have done it that way. But I did what I knew how to do at the time, and I paid for it with my job and with my New York State R.N.'s license."

"I'm sorry."

"It's a fucking crime the way people with AIDS have to suffer because of a profit-driven and corrupt homophobic health-care establishment in this country. That's a crime, not what I did." He went on with a speech to which I half listened and half thought about Aunt Moira's petunias out the window and the dull, sunny lives they lived.

When Rutka was through, I said, "Look, none of that makes up for the fact that Chief Bailey apparently has the goods on Eddie. Eddie has no alibi for the hour he was away from Kopy-King, and Mrs. Renfrew saw him in the yard. Bailey thinks you two planned the fire and, to tell you the truth, the evidence he's got makes a certain impression on me."

A long, tremulous sigh. "First of all," he said, "has anyone asked Eddie where he was at the time of the fire? Under our system of government—unless it was changed over the weekend and I didn't hear about it— under our constitutional system, a man has a right to examine the evidence against him. He has a right to face his accuser. And he is, of course, innocent until proven guilty in a court of law. So naturally I am a little fucking bit disturbed that the Chief of Police of Handbag is going around making accusations of criminal misconduct behind a citizen's back! It's fucking unconstitutional, is what it is!"

I found a bottle of aspirin atop the refrigerator, held the phone between my chin and shoulder, and managed to pop the little bottle's lid. "So what would Eddie say if he was asked to account for his whereabouts at the time of the fire? Can you put him on the line?" I filled a glass of water and gulped down the two aspirin.

"Oh, I can see now exactly what is going on here. Bailey told you this bullshit and now it sounds as if you agree with him and you're going to join him in his campaign to blame the victim."

I said, "That's enough."

"What?"

"I can't take this. Every word you speak gives me a headache and I've had enough. I resign."

"No, please!"

"I'll mail you back your check, John. I can't work for you. I think you lie as naturally as you eat candy, and I think both the shooting and the fire are stunts you and Eddie staged to get sympathy and attention for you and your cause. It's a good cause overall—it's my good cause, too—but you're going about it in a way that goes too far and hurts innocent people and is self-defeating. I can't participate, I'm sorry."

"But you agreed! You said you would help protect me for twenty-four hours and you're not keeping your promise. You can't leave me alone like this when I'm in real danger! It's unfair! Look, I know I've cut a few corners. Can you tell me you've never cut a corner or two for a good cause? No, no, you can't, I know it. And even if I am too assertive sometimes, and I step on a few toes that maybe I shouldn't, do I deserve to be murdered for it? This is fucking insane! This is unfair! This is—"

I hung up on him. I couldn't stand to hear him speak another word. I quickly disconnected the answering machine and plugged the phone line back into the wall outlet. A few seconds later, when the phone began to ring, I let it ring and ring. Then I wrote a note for Timmy and left the house.

10

"How is he?" I said.

"The same."

It was a quarter after eight that night and we were in the corridor outside room F-5912 at Albany Med.

"Is Mike in there?"

"Yes, and Rhoda and Al."

"I'll go in and say hello."

"Your note said you quit working for John Rutka. What happened?"

"You can guess."

"He's insufferable."

"That sums it up. It's not just his views, either. Those I can cope with or even agree with. He lies habitually."

"It wouldn't be the first time a client lied to you. Not that I mean to defend Rutka."

"I don't think he knows the difference between when he's lying and when he's not. It seems to be pathological."

Three nuns came out of room F-5913 across the corridor, where the bishop lay comatose, and Timmy gave them a friendly nod. "Did you get a look at the famous files?" he said.

"Yeah."

"Anything I should know about?"

"That's confidential investigator-client information."

"Ha-ha. Cough it up."

"Nothing much, really. The governor and his entire cabinet are transvestites who dress up in a basement room in the capitol every Thursday morning at eleven. The governor is Arlene Francis and the commissioner of corrections is Miss Kitty Carlisle."

"Oh, everybody knows that. It's why he'll never run for president."

"Other than that, there was nothing in the files you didn't already know, I'm pretty sure."

"That's probably true. So who shot Rutka?"

"I think he did it himself, or Sandifer did. It's their little bit of guerrilla theater. Their house was set on fire today and all the evidence points to their being responsible for that, too. The Handbag police chief just wants them to leave town, and at this point I think that's the best deal they're going to get and they should take it."

"Cripes, Rutka is even scuzzier than I thought."

The wife of the unconscious truck driver who shared the room with the bishop came out into the corridor looking red-eyed and defeated, and plodded toward the elevators.

"Rutka is pretty confused," I said. "It's surreal the way he mixes keen perceptions of real threats with screwy paranoid delusions. Me, I've had enough of it."

"So you're off the case entirely?"

"I'm returning his check. It's as if I was never on it. I've never done that with a client, but the guy was driving me nuts. I had such a headache this afternoon I drove out to Thatcher Park and ambled around in the woods for four hours to clear my head. It was lovely. I loafed and invited my soul."

"Did it show up?"

"Yes, and we had a nice exchange of views. I'm going to go in now and say hello to Mike and then go get something to eat. Have you eaten?"

"Sure, but I'll go with you. Mike has been bugging me and I have to go away and think about something."

"What?"

"You'll hear about it. You'll get it too."

I walked past the skinny, gape-mouthed man who never had any visitors and into Stu Meserole's curtained-off end of the room. Stu's father, Al, a gray-faced, middle-aged man in a windbreaker, was sprawled dozing in a small wooden armchair at the foot of Stu's bed. Rhoda Meserole, squat and pretty with fresh lipstick and a new perm, was seated in the folding chair alongside the bed and was massaging Stu's unresponsive right hand. Mike Sciola was perched on the stool on the other side of the bed and held Stu's limp left hand.

"Hi, Stu," I said quietly, and could hardly resist the urge to say it more loudly. Maybe he's not brain-dead, just hard of hearing, I thought, and we ought to be yelling in his ear, as if he were Reagan, and that would make him wake up: "HI, STU! HOPE YOU'RE FEELING BETTER AND ARE UP AND AROUND SOON!"

"It was nice of you to come, Donald," Mrs. Meserole said. It was what she always said. "As you can see, Stuart is still in his coma."

"I'm sorry."

"He's so peaceful."

"I want to talk to you before you leave," Mike said. "Are you in a hurry?"

"No."

"Why don't we go outside now?"

74

Rhoda Meserole smiled and lowered her eyelids, and her sleeping husband snored comfortably. Mike followed me into the corridor.

"This is the hardest thing I have ever had to do or will ever have to do," he said to me quietly. Timmy came over and listened. "I talked to the doctor today."

"Is there any hope at all?"

"He says no, there isn't. It's not that parts of Stu's brain are dead. It's that—parts of his brain aren't even there anymore." He began to choke up, then struggled and recovered himself. "There's no hope. He's gone. Stu is gone and that's his corpse in that room."

"I believe it. That's the way it feels to go in there."

"For a long time," he said, "I was afraid maybe Stu was alive inside that body and going crazy and screaming to die. I don't believe that anymore. The doctor explained some things to me about how the brain works, and the part of Stu's brain that could think like that is gone."

"Good."

"But the thing is— This is the thing." He started to breathe heavily again and struggled with his words. "I can't leave him there like that—a corpse in a bed with people pretending he's a living human being and pumping food into him. It's gruesome. It's an insult to Stu's dignity." He screwed up his face in disgust. I could see what was coming. I was surprised it hadn't come sooner.

"And the thing is," Mike went on, "I have to go back to school in three weeks. I have a contract. I'm obligated, and anyway I have no other means of support except for what I earn. So I have to go back. But the thing is"—he gave me a look of consuming desperation—"the thing is, I can't leave him like that."

I waited.

"Will you help me?"

He looked at me.

I had heard of situations such as this one, where rules, even laws, had been broken in order to do what was all but indisputably right and humane. But I'd never heard of it done in a hospital, except by physicians in collusion with the patient's legal caretaker, and never with the patient's family sitting guard nearby in order to prevent just such an eventuality.

"What could I do?" I finally said.

"I've figured out a way to do it," he said, sweating and weaving a little.

"What do you mean?"

"There's a little sort of trapdoor in the IV tubing. It's called a port. It's where nurses can inject drugs into the patient's bloodstream. If I had a drug, I could inject it in there. I could do it in ten seconds while Al is asleep and Rhoda is in the bathroom, and then Rhoda would come out of the bathroom and the plug would be in the wall socket, and the machinery would be humming, and everything would look normal. And soon Stu would drift away. 'He went so peacefully,' Rhoda could say. And then it would be over and we could remember the real Stu and miss him." His face contorted.

"I don't think you could get away with it," I said. "They'd do an autopsy and figure it out. They'd find the drug in him, and if they didn't come after you right away, they'd come down on some innocent nurse. There would be an investigation and the Meseroles would fuel the flames. If it was traced back to you, the Meseroles might try to have you prosecuted for God-knows-what—murder? You could lose your teaching job at a minimum."

"And your health benefits," Timmy added, not at all trivially, for we all knew what this eventually could mean for Mike himself.

"I've thought of all that," Sciola said. A nurse strode up

the hall and Mike waited until she had disappeared into the bishop's room. "The thing is," he said, leaning close to me, "is that an autopsy isn't done routinely. It's not required by law. I called the state and checked. If it's requested by the family, it's done, or maybe if the patient is part of a research project. Or if there are extraordinary circumstances of some kind. But that wouldn't be the case here. Here it's a man in a coma with half his brain gone and his heart stops and that's the end. It wouldn't be medically surprising."

I looked into Mike's face and stood there. "What makes you think I could get whatever it is you would need?"

"You're a detective. You have connections. You could find out how."

Timmy was shaking his head. "Stu is not suffering," he said. "He doesn't know about things like dignity anymore. It's an irrelevant consideration."

"Well then, what about *my* dignity?" Sciola said in a harsh whisper. "How much longer am *I* supposed to endure this stupid-bullshit-nightmare crap?"

The nurse came out of the bishop's room and rolled down the hall. We waited. "Death is undignified," Timmy said. "It's undignified being around it. There's no getting away from it. It's an indignity we all have to experience. In a life full of ridiculous indignities, it's the most ridiculous indignity of all."

"Are you objecting on religious grounds?" I asked Timmy.

"I thought you knew me better than that, Donald. The church will always have my heart, but I reclaimed my mind decades ago. No, I'm against it for the entirely practical reason that Mike might get caught and pay a price that's not worth it. If Stu were screaming in pain, maybe—okay, yes. But this is different. There's too much to lose for what it is you'd gain. I can see how awful you feel, Mike, but I'm afraid you'd regret it. Wait. See what happens. Stu's life is lost, but yours isn't. Don't risk it for something that, as you've already faced up to, is already gone."

Sciola glared at both of us, turned and fled back into the room.

I looked at Timmy. "Maybe I can do something," I said.

"Let's go get something for you to eat," he said. "Nobody has to decide anything right now."

"I'll just say good-bye to Mike."

"What are you going to say to him?"

"Nothing. Just good-bye."

"All right. I'm not your mother."

"Yes, you are."

I went into the room and Mike looked up and met my gaze. I nodded once. His eyes brightened and he nodded back. Mrs. Meserole said, "Thank you for coming, Donald," and I went out again.

Queequeg's had set up tables out on the sidewalk under a rickety canopy, and this meant it was possible to have a steak teriyaki platter and a beer while risking respiratory failure from the fumes of the New Scotland Avenue traffic or death from a stray bullet fired during a domestic quarrel in the apartment building across the street.

I was nonetheless chowing down happily, and Timmy was enjoying a small aperitif—we agreed not to discuss Mike Sciola's plea for the time being—when a colleague of Timmy's from the legislature came by and recognized us.

"Don, weren't you working for John Rutka? Somebody said he hired you."

"Briefly, I was. Why?"

"Didn't you hear?"

"Hear what? No."

"Rutka is dead. It was on the radio just now. He was killed in a fire tonight."

I stared at the man and couldn't think of a word to say.

11

We drove over to Crow Street. Timmy had re-hooked up the answering machine when he arrived home from work, and now there were two messages on it. Both were from Eddie Sandifer. The first, in a tremulous voice, said, "I think somebody took John. It looks like he was kidnaped. Please, I need your help. Call me at the house as soon as you can. I'm going to call the Handbag police." The second message, delivered in a monotone, said simply, "He's dead. John's dead and I don't know what to do."

I dialed Rutka's number in Handbag.

"Yell-o."

"Eddie?"

"This is Officer Hughs of the Handbag Police Department. Who do you want?"

"Edward Sandifer."

"Hold on."

Half a minute later, an all-but-lifeless voice: "Yes?"

"This is Strachey. What happened?"

"John's dead. Somebody killed him."

80

"That's— I can hardly believe it."

"I know."

"He was in a fire?"

"They took him from here and tied him up in an old house and burned it down."

"Oh, hell."

"Can you come out?"

"I'm surprised you want me to."

"I do. Please come out."

"I'll be there in twenty minutes. Do they have any idea who did it?"

"No. They keep questioning me. I don't know how much to say."

"How much to say about what?"

"Well, there are some things you should know."

"Uh-huh. Have the cops asked for the files?"

"They don't seem to know about them. They keep asking for the names of people who threatened John."

"Don't mention the files. I'll be out."

"Thank you. Please hurry."

We were on 787 North in three minutes with the windows down and the hot night air loud in our faces. My headache was back and I was unable to answer Timmy's questions.

"Was Sandifer there when Rutka was dragged away?"

"I don't know."

"Where was the fire?"

"In an old house. That's all I know."

"Was he badly burned? How do they know it was Rutka's body?"

"I don't know. I know what you're thinking."

"I guess they'll be thorough—the medical examiner. Whoever confirms the identification of the body."

"They tend to be. And in this case they'll be extra thorough."

A police cruiser turned out of Elmwood Place as we turned in, and as we pulled up in front of the house a second car made a U at the end of the block and came back down and out of the neighborhood.

"Are they gone?" Sandifer said as we came in the front door.

"They're gone. Who was here?"

"John's sister Ann and Bub Bailey and another policeman." He fell back against the wall, buried his face in his hands, and heaved, up and down.

After a time, I said, "You'd better sit down, Eddie," and led him by the arm into the living room, where he collapsed in a chair, snuffling. The charred odor from the morning fire on the back porch filled the house, and it was as if it was the stench of Rutka's remains.

"I'm sorry, Eddie. What can I tell you."

"Nothing. What can anybody say? Maybe I shouldn't have gone to work tonight and left him alone. But he said I should go ahead. And there wasn't anything he had to worry about. Not really."

"There wasn't?"

He looked up at me and let loose with something that was half sigh, half shudder. "Well, you abandoned him, and you didn't even know."

"Know what?"

"I mean, you didn't know for sure."

"What? That you threw the firebomb today and shot John in the foot last night?"

He glanced at Timmy. "He's okay," I said.

Sandifer looked away. "It was John's idea," he said in a tremulous voice, "not mine. I always told him gay people didn't have to pretend to be under attack from homophobes. All we had to do was go out in public and not hide the fact we were gay and sooner or later we'd get our faces punched in, if that's what he wanted to

82

prove. But he said there was never enough evidence, or gay people were afraid to report it, or the cops would ignore it—if they weren't the ones doing the beating themselves. So sometimes you had to do 'a little reality-based charade,' was how John put it. Shooting him in the foot last night practically made me want to throw up."

"Staging a fag-bashing does seem a little redundant these days," I said. "And what was my role supposed to be in all this? Why was I lied to and manipulated and conned into the scam? To lend credibility?"

He flushed and couldn't look up at me. "That and to get feedback from the cops. John thought they'd tell you things they wouldn't tell him. And he thought all the people who had threatened him would really be freaked if they thought you might be coming after them."

I felt a rush of fury at Rutka for being dead and not available for me to get my hands around his throat. I said, "You two lunkheads sure botched the whole thing real good, didn't you? You got away with the shooting last night, so far, but your neighbor spotted you on your way to toss the bomb today. Have you confessed to the police?"

His head jerked up. "No! Jesus! I don't want to go to prison. Anyway, now there really is a killer."

"And once he's identified, he might as well take the rap for the two unsuccessful attempts, is that it?"

"Well—why not? Oh, I don't know. What difference does it make? What difference does *anything* make anymore!"

I said, "Have they identified the body? Are they sure it was John? What happened?"

He started to speak, then wept again. After a moment, he said, "They're pretty sure it's John they found. They'll know for sure tomorrow. Oh, God, it's real, this time! This time it's really real!"

"So you weren't here when it happened?"

He snuffled some more and then said, "I went in to work to finish up some things I didn't get to this morning when I was—you know—out for a while. It was around six-thirty when I went in. John had gotten a call earlier, the one he told you about, saying this time he was going to burn. And at first it freaked us both out, but then he said, shit, he'd gotten lots of threats and none of them ever amounted to anything, so let's forget it. So we did.

"When I got back from the shop a little after eight, I came in and John wasn't here and a chair in the dining room was knocked over and the table was pushed back with the rug all bunched up. It looked like there had been a struggle or fight and John had been kidnaped. I was really scared all of a sudden, and I called you and you weren't home, and then I called the police. They sent a cruiser out, but as soon as the cop got here he got a call on his radio about the fire and he just took off."

"You'd gone into Albany in your car?"

"In John's. It's the one we use. I don't have a car. It's the Subaru back in the garage."

"Where was the fire?"

"Down behind Pocketbook Factory Number Three," he said, and took out a bandanna and wiped his mouth and nose. "There are some abandoned houses down there that belonged to the pocketbook company. Whoever started the fire used a lot of gasoline or something and the place went up like a fireball, Bub Bailey said."

"And John's body was badly burned?"

Sandifer shook and started to lose it again. "They could tell it was John because his wallet was left on the curb out front with a note in it. And from his wounded foot and— they're going to check on other things, dental records and things like that. Ann told them which dentist." He blew his nose in the bandanna.

84

"What did this note say that was stuck in the wallet?"

"They showed it to me but they kept it and they kept the wallet. It was horrible. The note said—it was printed in big letters on a piece of typing paper—it said, 'This is what happens to assholes who invade people's privacy.'"

"That's plain enough. It tends to confirm the motive."

"Why else would anybody do it?" Sandifer said. "Who else would want to kill John?"

"Can you think of anyone?"

"No, it must have been one of the people he outed. Or more than one of them. They'd've had to drag John out of here. He had a gun and he wouldn't have gone without a struggle. Maybe there were two, or even three or four."

"Where is the gun now?"

"I haven't seen it. I'll have to look."

"Did the police question the neighbors?"

"Chief Bailey went around himself. He said nobody saw or heard any fight or anything violent."

I said, "What are these, pod people around here? Nobody comes or goes, or sees or hears anything."

"They're elderly," Sandifer said. "They stay in with their air conditioners and their televisions on."

"What did you tell Bailey about the threats John received? You can be sure he'll question everybody who ever threatened John to find out where they were tonight—and last night when John was shot in the foot, and this morning at the time of the fire. You might even get Bailey believing that the other so-called attempts were real. I guess I'm glad you told me the truth, but I'm not crazy about knowing your dirty little politically-far-too-correct secret and having to pretend to Bub Bailey that I don't."

Timmy, who had sat silently scowling through my en-

85

tire exchange with Sandifer, suddenly piped up. "I'm not crazy about being in on it either."

This was why I hardly ever brought him along on business. Tonight had been a lapse. I said, "But now you are in on it, so let's just get on with the more important questions."

He looked away in disgust.

I said to Sandifer, "What names did you give Bailey?"

"Just the ones on the list John made up of people who threatened him—Slinger and Linkletter and those. And I gave him a complete set of *Cityscapes* and *Queerscreeds* with John's outing columns. I didn't mention any of the anonymous calls though, or all the people in the files. Do you think I should have brought them up?"

"No. I'll deal with those."

This got Timmy's attention again. "What do you mean?"

"I'll use the files. There's no reason for the police to have to go into them if I'm covering that end of the investigation." He gave me a look. "The files are obviously the key to finding John's killer or killers. And since it's important that they not fall into the hands of a government agency that might misuse them—as police agencies almost inevitably will—then I'll just have to take possession of the files and use them to find the killer and turn him—or them—over to the police with enough evidence to convict."

"Will you do that?" Sandifer said, looking a little brighter. "God, that would be great."

"Don—" Timmy said, and then realizing he could not say what he wanted to say in front of Sandifer, he waved it away.

"I don't have any choice," I said, "as far as I can see. It's either turn the files over to the cops, which is out of the question, or use them as an investigative tool at least as effectively as the police would. What else can I do?"

86

"Maybe you should just turn them over," Timmy said uneasily. "It's the Handbag police who'd be looking at them, not the much more dangerous Albany cops. Anyway, anybody who's in those files must have done so many disgusting things that the police already have them on their lists of the region's most outrageous perverts."

"I can't believe you said that."

"Well, you know what I mean."

Sandifer said, "They do tend to be the biggest whores. Most of those people didn't get into the files without being real scuzzballs."

"Scuzzballs deserve their privacy too," I said, "the Burger Court's loony Five Stooges 1986 opinion to the contrary notwithstanding. Anyway, I happen to have read through those files this morning, and I can tell you that most of the people in there are simply gay men and women who live Ozzie-and-Harriet lives with their significant others, more or less, and a few of whom have strayed once in a while and their indiscretions happen to have been picked up and noted by some of John Rutka's informants. Should that information become official police information?"

"No," Timmy said, "of course not." He had on a distant thoughtful look, as if this were an interesting theoretical question concerning the abstract gay masses.

"John would be grateful," Sandifer said, and began to grow teary again. "He's always sort of expected to be disappointed in the people he's counted on. It was years before he even trusted me totally. It would have mattered a lot that you stuck by him, Strachey."

Timmy sat there with a quizzical look, as if unsure how I had managed to end up taking on work that would help serve as a memorial to a man Timmy had considered rotten to the core and whom I hadn't been too crazy about either. Whatever my degree of responsibility or lack of it in John Rutka's death—I didn't have the will or the energy to think about that quite yet—I was still obliged to stay on the case for one very good reason: as soon as I found the killer I could burn the loathsome files.

I said, "We'd better haul the files out of here and over to Crow Street, where I can lock them up." Timmy winced. "Eddie, maybe you'd better come too. You're probably in no danger, but you'll be able to feel secure in our spare room, and anyway I might need you to answer some questions about the files."

"Yeah, okay. I don't want to stay here alone tonight. I don't want to sleep alone in that room."

In the teenaged girl's bedroom on the second floor, Sandifer reached into the hippo's belly for the attic keys. He groped around, then shook the animal, vigorously, and then frantically.

"The keys aren't here."

We tore out to the attic door, which hung open. The keys dangled in the upper of the two locks. The light was on in the airless attic but the fan was off, as if someone had been there briefly and then left in a hurry. The desk and file cabinet appeared undisturbed, except that the top file drawer had been pulled out. It did not have a ransacked look, however. I said, "I suppose there's no way to tell if a file has been removed, or is there?"

"The index," Sandifer said, and opened the top drawer of the desk. He removed a bundle of papers clipped together and said, "We'll have to go through both drawers and check the files against the list. Do you think whoever took John made him open the files first and took his own out?"

"His or theirs. That's what it looks like."

"Jesus. Then all we have to do to find out who did it is to see whose file is missing."

"Maybe. Though a killer who's playing with a full deck

88

would have thought of the possibility of an index to the files and would have taken them all. Or he'd have taken someone else's file to aim the investigation in the wrong direction."

"Maybe he's not that smart," Sandifer said, and I hoped he was right. Although it was soon apparent that whether the pilferer of the files was brilliant or stupid hardly mattered at all.

12

"There's no name on this entry," Timmy said. "It just says 'A for All-American Asshole Mega-Hypocrite.'"

"Who's that?" I asked Sandifer. "What does he mean by 'A for—whatever-it-is Mega-Hypocrite'?"

"'A for All-American Asshole Mega-Hypocrite,'" Timmy said again.

Sandifer looked baffled. "I don't know. I have no idea."

"All the other names in the index are spelled out," Timmy said. "Mega-Hypocrite is the only one that's coded like that."

We were back in Albany and had the file cabinet in the spare room in the second-floor rear of our house on Crow Street. The top drawer was open and I was checking the actual files against the index Timmy was reading from. The first name on the "A" page had been "Anderson, Cliff," and the file had been in the front of the drawer where it should have been. But when I looked for the second folder, for All-American Asshole Mega-Hypocrite, it was not in the drawer.

"All-American Mega-Hypocrite is missing. Or maybe it's misfiled."

"I would doubt it," Sandifer said. "There were some things John could be careless about, but not record-keeping. He was meticulous."

I searched through the files, in case Mega-Hypocrite had slid down or been uncharacteristically misplaced somehow.

"How would anybody stealing the file know that All-American Mega-Hypocrite was his designation?" Timmy said. "Eddie doesn't even know what it meant."

"Dunno. He might have forced Rutka to tell him which one was his file. We can assume he didn't know about the index in the desk drawer or he would have taken it. Or, he might have checked the files for a folder under his own name and, when he didn't find one, started a random search. He'd have come to the All-American Mega-Hypocrite file right away, maybe seen that the shoe fit, and verified it by going through the actual contents of the file."

I kept flipping through the folders, eyes peeled for Mega-Hypocrite. I asked Sandifer if there were any of the outees or soon-to-be-outees Rutka considered to be especially repugnantly hypocritical. "Bruno Slinger maybe?"

"He considered them all sickeningly hypocritical," Sandifer said. "The worst one was always the one he was going after during whatever week it was."

Rutka's column in the next planned *Queerscreed,* galleys of which we had carried off from his desktop, outed an independently wealthy ACLU booster, not much of a candidate for Mega-Hypocrite.

Timmy said, "If they weren't *for* the cause, they were against it, eh?" He was gripping the index sheaf tightly, and I was glad it wasn't a club.

"Sort of," Sandifer said. "I guess you could put it that way."

"Righteous John Rutka and the unrighteous multitudes."

"Timothy," I said, reminding him with a look that it was all moot now.

"Actually," Sandifer said, "there was this one person, I know, who John had been working on for a long time trying to get the goods on. He knew the guy was gay but he didn't have the proof, or enough proof. He never told me who it was because he said I'd never believe it."

"Why wouldn't you have believed it? Didn't you trust John?"

Sandifer flushed and gave a quick embarrassed shrug. "John was sometimes loose with some of his facts."

"Even with you?"

"He just couldn't help it. I realized this about him not long after we met. But it was just the way he was and I got used to it. He mostly just made things up about himself, not other people. I don't think he was ever dishonest in his work. He would never say it, but I think he knew he'd been able to maintain his professional integrity and he was proud of that. And he was always careful in his outing columns to get his facts right."

"What else did he tell you about this special case? Could this be our Mr. A-for-All-American Asshole Mega-Hypocrite?"

"I can't remember. I don't think he said anything else about the guy. The only reason I remember at all," Sandifer said, "is because John got a kind of funny, intense look when he mentioned it. I can remember the day. We were in the car driving up the street in Handbag and he told me about this guy he said he was really going to fix, and he had this look on his face I'd never seen before. I can still see him."

"Describe the look."

"Just weird, intense. And I think he might have been blushing a little. Or maybe just angry. I don't know what it was."

"Mega-Hypocrite is nowhere in the top drawer," I said. I started through the bottom drawer.

Timmy had been flipping idly through the index sheets, perusing the names, and clucking in mild disgust. *"What!"*

He'd been perched on the edge of the guest room bed and suddenly he rose straight up like a Looney Tunes character. He went into a swivet, hit the ceiling, went through the roof. "Did you *see* this?"

"What's that?"

"I'm in here! My name is in the index!"

"Now do you agree it's better that I deal with the files and they don't fall into the hands of the police?"

"Let me see the file. Look in the *C*'s."

"I didn't know," Sandifer said. "Jeez, I'm really sorry."

I handed Timmy the folder with his name on it and said, "This is a pretty slender dossier for a pervert as outrageous as yourself."

He read it. "This is disgusting. It's from a hotel employee who says— Oh, crime-en-ee."

I kept on flipping through the bottom drawer searching for Mega-Hypocrite.

"Have you seen this?" he said, moaning.

"I have."

"That liar."

"It's always risky placing your trust in economists."

"He told me he'd never done it before with a North American."

"And did the earth move?"

"I guess you two have a pretty open relationship," Sandifer said. "John and I did for a while, but everything started to come apart, so we went back to monogamy."

"Our rules are variable," I said. "Well, no, that's not quite it."

Timmy snapped, "He means it's not the rules that are variable, it's the observance of them. Recently, only by me. I made a mistake once in fourteen years. And look at this putrid bilge! I would not feel any more violated and demeaned if I discovered this garbage in the files of the F.B.I. In fact, this is worse. I can't believe that gay people are doing this to other gay people. This is not a blow against the old-fashioned fear and self-loathing that made gay people miserable through the supposedly recently ended dark ages—it's just a kind of bizarre extension of it."

Sandifer was sitting in a chair with his head in his hands and saying nothing. Timmy looked over at him and said, "I guess I've made my point. I'll shut up. You don't need to be listening to this now."

"It's okay," Sandifer said dolefully. "It doesn't matter what anybody says anymore."

I said, "There's no Mega-Hypocrite file in here. Assuming that such a file actually existed, somebody seems to have taken pains to excise it."

Timmy shoved the "T. Callahan" file back my way as if it were soiling his hands and said, "Why wouldn't it have existed?"

"Rutka could have planned a file by that name, then changed his mind and used the hypocrite's real name instead. A name on one of the other files might be the real Mega-Hypocrite."

"So maybe one of the other files is missing. We haven't checked that."

"Let's do it."

It took two and a half minutes for Timmy to read off each of the 311 names in the index. A file was located for each name. The files were flawlessly arranged in alphabetical order. Still, the only file missing was the one called "A for All-American Asshole Mega-Hypocrite."

Sandifer suddenly looked alert. He said, "Maybe the books would help."

We looked at him. "Books?"

"John kept financial records for the whole outing campaign in *Cityscape* and *Queerscreed*. Sometimes he paid people for information. That's not the ideal way to go about it, I know, but John always believed that ethically these things evened themselves out over the long run."

"Where are these financial records?"

"In my bag. I brought them. I didn't think I should leave them alone in the house."

"Where's the bag?"

"In the hall." He went out and came back immediately carrying a big beat-up red shoulder bag stuffed with belongings. He unzipped it, reached in and groped around, and came up with a bookkeeper's bound entry book.

"How is this going to help?" Timmy said.

"Maybe it won't. But if Rutka had informants who dished up dirt that was so critical to the cause that Rutka was willing to lay out cash for it, maybe one of those people can figure out—or will know—who the Mega-Hypocrite is."

I scanned the ledger. Rutka seemed to have had just one source of income, the family hardware store. "HDW" brought in from three thousand to four thousand dollars each month. I asked Sandifer if Rutka had owned half the store.

"Forty-nine percent. Ann owns fifty-one. That's the way it was left to them by their father."

"John didn't resent the difference?"

"He was interested in the income, not the control. Ann

runs the store for a good salary and does a good job. And the two of them got along in their way. They were different but they never got in each other's way. John lived his life and Ann lived hers."

The disbursements included household expenses—utilities, taxes, locksmith—along with occasional "personal" disbursements, and larger ones for "office and printing." Most of the payments in the latter category were made to Kopy-King. There was no category called "informants" or "spies" or "dish."

There were, however, payments to three entries listed apparently by their initials: NZ, DR, and JG. I'd never seen NZ or DR before, but JG I had. I got out Ronnie Linkletter's file and there it was: the handwritten sheet Rutka had left that said "From JG—Linkletter at motel with A." Then two long rows of dates. I checked the calendar and saw that they were all Wednesdays, starting the previous July and running into mid-June.

I asked Sandifer if he knew what these initials meant. He puzzled over them and finally said no. The "A" might have meant Asshole Mega-Hypocrite, but the other initials, if that's what they were, remained indecipherable.

I read aloud the payments to NZ: $320 in December; $435 in January; $310 in February; similar amounts through July. JG received even higher amounts from October through July, totaling nearly $6,000. DR was the big money-maker. He—or she, or it—was paid an even $1,400 per month from the previous September right up through July. According to a notation in the margin, all these payments had been made "in cash."

I asked Sandifer, "Were you ever with John when he met his regular informants? It looks as if that's what these entries refer to. He could have received information from them over the phone, but he must have met them once a month to hand over the cash payments for their diligent

96

research. People in their right minds don't send cash amounts larger than a dime through the mail these days."

"No, I never did. John would just say he had to go talk to somebody. Or he had a meeting with somebody. He wanted to keep me out of that part of it. To protect me, was what he said."

"Protect you from what? You were out in the streets hustling *Queerscreed*. Wasn't that where the greatest physical risk was?"

"I guess so. I'm not sure what he meant by that—protecting me. I guess he thought some of the people he was after and some of the people they were mixed up with were dangerous. And he was right," Sandifer added with eyes glistening. "John knew somehow that some of them were very dangerous people."

I could no longer argue with that.

13

The three of us were in the kitchen the next morning at seven.

"I'll make a few calls while Timmy goes through his Donna Reed routine," I told Sandifer.

"Who's that?"

"She was one of the great chefs of the middle part of the century," Timmy said. "Would you like some eggs? That's what Donald eats."

"Sure."

"He used to drink them, blended with orange juice, but now they've all got salmonella and cleaning up the chicken industry would be communistic. Not that the Communists ever cleaned up theirs."

"I'd like mine fried on both sides with nothing runny anywhere."

"That's a good precaution to take."

I dragged the phone into the cubbyhole under the front stairs, shut the door, and phoned Bub Bailey. He was in his office early, as I expected he might be.

"I gave John Rutka your advice, Chief, but he didn't take it."

"No, I feel real bad for the boy. He had a hard life and he died in a way nobody should have to. It's a blessing Charlie and Doris are gone and don't have to see this."

"What do you mean, John had a hard life? I wouldn't have thought of it that way."

"I don't mean to say he was disadvantaged or he'd been abused. John was always just a big, odd, nice-looking kid who told tales and never fit in very well. His mom and dad never knew quite what to make of him. It was good when John went off to find himself in the city. I admired the boy for coming home when Charlie and Doris went into their decline, but after they died I could never figure out why John stayed on."

"Has the body been positively identified?"

"No, I should hear by noon, the M.E. says. I told him—I suggested he be extra certain on this one."

"That went through my mind, too."

"The circumstantial evidence was there, the wallet and the note. And a body that was the right size and sex—what was left of it. It was a sickening sight. There was little left of John besides the chains that bound him."

"Chains?"

"At the wrists and ankles, and padlocked. There's no way that boy could have gotten loose. He wouldn't have suffered from the fire, though. The preliminary exam showed he'd been shot in the head. This will all be in the paper, by the way, so I'm not giving anything away here that I shouldn't. Though, come to think of it, maybe there's something you could help me out with."

"What's that, Chief?"

"I talked to a colleague on the Albany force last night who keeps his ear to the ground down there, and he says John was supposed to have kept files on all the people he wrote about or was planning to write about in his column, and these files were supposed to have all kinds of dope in them about who's gay in Albany. Do you know anything about this?"

"I've heard that story too."

"But you have no firsthand knowledge of these files?"

"I would hope that any such files would have gone up in flames with their keeper. It's an abominable thing to have created."

"That doesn't answer my question, Mr. Strachey. Do you know about the files and where they might be located? As you know, these files could be critical in investigating John's murder."

I grasped the receiver tightly and said, "John mentioned the files, Chief, but he never showed them to me or told me where he kept them. They're probably at his house. Have you searched it?"

"I'm heading over there soon, but I can't seem to get hold of Edward Sandifer. Do you know whether he's still in the Rutka house?"

"No, he's not. I picked him up last night and brought him into Albany."

"Yes, I saw your car."

"He's staying with a friend—on Washington Avenue, I think he said. I dropped him off at Johnny's Hot Dogs on Central around eleven-thirty."

"Well, this complicates matters. I asked him to be available and he hasn't done it. If you speak to Sandifer, tell him to phone me immediately. I'll need access to the house for a thorough search, and questions are bound to come up."

"Maybe Ann could let you into the house. She'd probably have a key, wouldn't she?"

"She may well. I'll check."

"Chief, I'd like to think that whoever killed John is not an immediate threat to other people, but I know that anybody who has killed once is capable of killing again. So good luck to you."

"You're not going to interfere with my investigation, are you, Mr. Strachey? When I mentioned your name, my colleague in Albany said you would probably interfere. He put it less politely than that."

"No, I'm not going to get in your way, Chief. I might ask around some, and if I come up with anything I'll certainly pass the information on to you."

"Well, I would certainly expect you to."

"I'll dig up what little I can," I said. "Have you checked Rutka's wallet for prints yet? And what about prints on the note left with the wallet?"

"Yes, that would be standard procedure in an investigation of this type. The note and the wallet are on their way to the state lab for analysis."

"The note seems to rule out any motive except revenge for Rutka's outing campaign. What was it the note said?"

" 'This is what happens to, uh, quote, assholes, unquote, who invade people's privacy.' Yes, the motive is clear enough. Unless the note was supposed to steer investigators away from the real motive. We have to remain alert to that possibility."

"True. Has any other motive suggested itself yet?"

"No. John seems to have made an awful lot of people mad enough to kill him. But they were all mad at him for the same reason. That's why it's imperative that I get hold of those files he's supposed to have kept. My suspicion is that the files will turn out to be the key to the investigation. You're sure you know nothing about them?"

"I'm afraid not."

"Well, I believe you. You have the reputation of being an honest man, Mr. Strachey. And meeting you yesterday only confirmed that reputation in my mind."

"Thanks. Having your confidence is something I value, Chief."

"Let's stay in touch."

"We'll do that."

101

I hung up, grimacing, grateful no mirror was nearby to look into. Was I turning into John Rutka? "Ethically these things evened themselves out over the long run." Could you catch bad character from a client? Or had I done this before? It felt too familiar.

Now I had another call to make, and this one would be easier. Gay Albany—unlike, say, gay Istanbul—is composed largely of otherwise conventional middle-class male and female couples whose lives center around, not Queer Nation actions, but work, ordering from seed catalogs, and motoring over to Schenectady to see touring companies of *Cats* and *Les Miz*.

Like straight Albany, however, gay Albany has its racier underside, and as with straight Albany, there's a certain amount of traffic back and forth between respectable Albany and not-so-respectable Albany. I was among those who loved unrespectable gay Albany back in the years before it could kill you, and for both professional and nostalgic reasons I maintained connections to some of its more accomplished living practitioners. It was one of those I phoned now, to set up an appointment for later in the morning.

Back in the kitchen, Timmy was finishing up his porridge and tea and Sandifer his eggs. I ate mine cold.

"I spoke with Bub Bailey," I told Sandifer, "and he wants to get in touch with you. You might want to show up out at the house today. There's no need to mention you spent the night here. I told him you were with a friend on Washington Avenue."

"That's cool."

"He got wind of the files, or at least that such files exist. I said I'd heard that, too, but didn't know anything about them. How will you handle this when Bailey asks?"

"I don't know. What should I say? Should I lie?"

"You'll have to. We're stuck with that for now."

102

Timmy got up, flung his napkin on the table, and left the room.

"Is he pissed off?"

"He'll get over it. This is hard for him. It's not how he operates."

"He's strange."

"Maybe you could just tell Bailey the files used to be in the house but that John moved them after he was threatened and he didn't say where. How's that?"

"Okay."

The phone rang and I picked it up. It was Joel McClurg, editor of *Cityscape,* the paper Rutka wrote for until he started outing well-known non-ogres.

"Strachey, did you hear about John Rutka?"

"He died in a fire, I know. It's awful."

"I heard you were working for him and you might have some ideas on what's behind this. I'd like to send my reporter over to talk to you."

"Sure, but I won't be able to tell him much. The Handbag police know as much as I do."

"Sure they do. What kind of work were you doing for Rutka?"

"Well, that's confidential, Joel. I'm sure you understand that."

"Strachey, the bastard is dead. This would be on background. We wouldn't quote you."

I said, "Rutka had been threatened and shot in the foot, and yesterday his house was firebombed. He hired me to protect him."

"Nice job."

"Listen, you dealt with the guy. Did you believe half the things he said about himself?"

"No, maybe ten percent. But he was careful with what he wrote about other people. I did random checks of his sources and they were good."

"He was also a true believer and ruthless con artist for the cause. I got some background on him and the way he operated. I concluded the attacks on him in Handbag were staged and I dropped him, and then somebody killed him. I made my choice according to the evidence I had and it turned out I was wrong."

"I'm sorry. That's all you know?"

"That's about it."

"What about his files? I know he kept dossiers on all these people he was after for their hypocritical ways. Where are the files now?"

"I don't know. Nobody seems to be able to locate them. The Handbag cops were asking me, but I was no help. Eddie Sandifer doesn't even know. You know how neurotic Rutka could be."

"Well, I'd hate to see all that garbage fall into the wrong hands."

"You said it. Now that I've been forthcoming with you, maybe you can help me out, Joel. I told Bub Bailey, the Handbag police chief, that I'd pass on any information I came across that might help in the investigation. Here's a question you might be able to answer without breaking any rules of journalistic ethics."

"Go ahead."

"When Rutka was writing for you, did he ever mention anybody he considered a lot worse than the other people he was outing? Somebody he might have considered the biggest hypocrite of all?"

Without hesitation, McClurg said, "As a matter of fact, he did. I was going to mention it to you. As soon as I heard Rutka had been killed, I remembered this conversation we had last fall. We were sitting around in my office late one day after he brought his copy in. John told me there was somebody he wanted to get who was so evil—that's the word he used—so evil that he would do almost anything to expose this guy. But he was having trouble getting the goods on him, and he was feeling pretty frustrated."

"He gave you no clue at all who it was?"

"Just that it was someone who had connections with other people he said he was trying to out. He said he might be able to get this guy by way of the others. Not long after that we had our philosophical differences and parted company and I never heard any more about it. It might have been one of the local celebrities he did a job on later in *Queerscreed,* but I can't imagine who. The weatherman? The insurance agent? None of these people struck me as coming close to the epitome of evil. That's why we disagreed and I had to drop his column."

"But the evil one came back to you when you heard John had been killed."

"Maybe I'm just being melodramatic, but it was the first thing that hit me. One thing Rutka said did it. He said that if he somehow managed to nail this one, he didn't know what might happen."

"To him?"

"That's how I took it. He was always so cocky. But when he talked about this one, he seemed less sure of himself. He seemed scared. So maybe he was closing in on the guy and the evil one saw him coming and killed him."

"Are you going to put that in the paper?"

"I'm hoping my reporter will be smart enough to interview me. If he isn't, as his editor I'll suggest that he do so."

"When will your next edition be out?"

"Not for a week. Rutka's timing on this was poor for a weekly like ours. When the *T-U* calls to interview me, I won't bring this up if they don't ask. Or maybe even if they do. And the television bozos won't be interested.

They hate this. The whole thing cuts too close to the bone for them and could affect revenues. But pass it on to the Handbag cops if you want to. Or they can call me."

"I'll pass it on."

"You're not working on this on your own, are you, Strachey? That wouldn't be out of character."

"I'm helping out where I can, but that's all."

"I can imagine what that means. Well, when you're about to pounce on the killer, let me come along, will you? We've never had an exclusive on a homicide arrest before."

"Sure thing, Joel. But don't count on me. I'm way out on the periphery of this one."

He laughed and hung up. He doubted my word and I knew why. Temporarily I had become John Rutka, but after I solved the murder and destroyed the files I could become myself again. That was my plan.

14

The 8:25 A.M. "Hometown Folks" news insert on Channel Eight led with the story on John Rutka's death. A reporter stood in front of the smoke rising from the charred ruins of a house near the pocketbook factory and announced that police had tentatively identified a body found in the rubble as that of "controversial gay activist John Rutka." A fireman showed up to make the obligatory statement that the house had been "fully involved" when the firefighters arrived and to label the blaze "suspicious." Timmy had already left for work and wasn't there to ask, "What was the fire suspicious of?"

Bub Bailey appeared briefly to say that Rutka had been reported kidnaped earlier in the evening and that additional evidence pointed to foul play. A full investigation was being launched, he said.

Other stories on the "Hometown Folks" news-quickie concerned a full-landfill crisis in a Greene County town where residents had begun to heap their garbage in the town supervisor's elderly mother's front yard; a statement from recent U.S. Second Circuit Appeals Court

107

nominee and former Albany State football star Emmett "Pincher" Goerlach insisting that his remark in a 1989 speech to the Albany Rotary Club urging mandatory HIV testing for all unmarried Americans was "taken out of context" by its ACLU critics; and an elementary school in Watervliet that was raising money to send a bird with a broken wing to the Mayo Clinic.

Ronnie Linkletter, shoved from the heights of six and eleven after being outed in *Queerscreed*, came on for a quick do-si-do in front of a weather map that had a big winking smile face over the Northeast. This meant it would be sunny. I studied Linkletter's boyish face for signs of stress or anxiety but could discern none. His seemed to be as carefree and unrevealing as the smile face on the map.

Sandifer watched the news with me. When the report on the fire and Rutka's death came on, he slid into despondency and then shifted around and grew suddenly angry when Ronnie Linkletter appeared.

"He could be the one," Sandifer said. "He was one of the people who told John he was going to get him for what he did, and he could be the one who did it."

"He could."

I dialed around to the other area stations but had missed their local reports. The Schenectady PBS outlet was on the air even at this early hour with its pledge-week team and a fund-raising festival of June Allyson—Jimmy Stewart movies and reruns of *The Bell Telephone Hour*. The station was advertising a repeat showing of a Kingston Trio concert for its hipper viewers.

I brought the *Times Union* in from the front stoop. Because of the paper's earlier deadline, its report on Rutka and the fire was even sketchier than Channel Eight's had been. In the *T-U*, Rutka was a CHA, a "controversial homosexual activist."

108

I drove Sandifer out to Handbag so that he could check in with Bub Bailey and tell him some lies. We coordinated our stories on the way out. I would not have thought of myself as so skillful a dissembler as John Rutka, but it was I who took the lead in contriving a scenario for the loss of the files. The well-practiced Sandifer slid right into the routine.

Five messages were on Rutka's answering machine when Sandifer checked it. Bub Bailey asked Sandifer to phone him as soon as Sandifer got in. A *Times Union* reporter asked for a callback. Ann Rutka informed Sandifer that the funeral would be in two days, on Saturday, at nine-thirty, at St. Michael's in Handbag. There would be no calling hours at the funeral home. And two Queer Nation friends of Sandifer's and Rutka's phoned, both angry and distraught. One suggested an action to protest "gay genocide."

Sandifer reached Bub Bailey, who said he'd like to speak with Eddie and would drive over to the house. I listened while Sandifer ranted on cue to the *T-U* reporter. He managed to bring Ronald Reagan into his remarks about Rutka's murder in Handbag, as well as George Bush, and of course the fiend Ed Koch. It was as if Sandifer was trying to say what Rutka himself would have had to say about his own murder but he couldn't get it quite right. Or maybe he duplicated exactly what Rutka's spiel would have been. There wasn't any way to know.

At eleven-thirty I was back in Albany. I left the car in Washington Park and hiked over to State Street and the row of elegant turn-of-the-century manses that lined the northern edge of the park. Like most of the houses in the row, the big redstone Victorian castle I approached had been cut up into apartments for the bureaucrats and

109

professionals who had long since replaced the rich merchants and Democratic machine hacks as Albany's lifeblood. The rents were high, the address correct, and the view splendid, of the leas and copses in Frederick Law Olmsted's upstate vast green gem. The park was lovely and enduring, having survived even Nelson Rockefeller's attempt in the 1960s to run an interstate highway through it, and so detracting in a small way from the late governor's success as the Godzilla of urban design.

I pressed the button over a name in a recessed entryway that once must have been the servants' entrance.

"Yo?"

"It's Strachey."

A buzzer sounded and I pulled open a heavy oak door with an etched-glass window. I slid the gate open on the ancient two-passenger Otis, shoved it shut behind me, and pushed the button for four. The door to the sole top-floor apartment had been left open a crack and I went in and shut the door behind me.

"Hey, Strachey."

"Scotty."

He motioned and I followed him through the apartment with its marble and mirrors and silk flowers and gray leather couches. Scott S. Scott was barefoot and otherwise clad only in blue nylon running shorts and red suspenders—his brunch costume, I guessed. His classically proportioned physique was flawless except for a barely perceptible incipient bulge at the sides, and his tan had been evenly applied, the kind you might expect to see on a movie star of the 1950s or a Kennedy.

I said, "I thought only Larry King wore suspenders like that anymore."

"Well, I get a lot of customers who are nostalgic for the eighties."

He led me out onto a rooftop garden that was shielded

from sight by high hedges, and we sat under a honey-suckle-covered trellis alive with bees slurping nectar.

"Can I get you a Bloody Mary? Some blow?"

"Is that iced tea in that pitcher?"

"No, I think that's beer from last night."

"Thanks, I'll pass."

"The kid who cleans up hasn't come in yet."

I said, "Any problems with the help these days?"

I had met Scott S. Scott four years earlier, when he hired me to look into allegations by several of his customers that one of the male prostitutes he employed was attempting to blackmail well-off, deeply closeted customers. I identified the self-starter and arranged for his transportation to Southern California, where he later became vice president of a television home-shopping network.

Scott said, "No, the boys are cool. They know I won't put up with shit. And I'm more careful now who I hire. I run background checks. I want guys from stable homes who preferably attend church. Would you be interested in doing some background work? I use the Fricker Agency, but sometimes they get sloppy."

"Backgrounders are a little unexciting for me at this stage of the game, Scott. I guess not."

"Of course, so much of my business now is electronic. And for that you don't need good character. The business is changing."

"You mean phone sex?"

"I have a suite of offices over in Corporate Woods. You should drop in sometime, Strachey, and see my operation. I advertise in *Outweek*, the *Native*, the *Advocate*, and the rest. The color glossies of the hunks come from an agency in L.A. and cost me an arm and a leg. But I've got this roomful of trolls over by the interstate I pay six bucks an hour to, while the callers cough up a buck

111

a minute. You don't need choirboys for an operation like this. Just some horny old farts who'll show up on time and talk dirty for eight hours. With the labor surplus around here, it's like printing money."

"I don't suppose you have to worry about the Japanese competition."

"Hey, don't bet the farm on it. I was up to tar and feather my broker the other night and he was telling me how the Japs are getting into female retail sex in Mexico now. They've got whorehouses in Baja and Guadalajara where you can go down in the early evening and see the women doing calisthenics and marching up and down and singing the company song."

"I guess you were speaking metaphorically when you said you went up to tar and feather your broker. Or were you?"

"I do it at his place in Saratoga. He has a pool, and a grill where we can heat the tar. Not to boiling, the way they used to in the olden days. Just so it's soft enough to apply. Weird, huh? It's how he gets off. I go up once a week when his wife's down shopping in the city, and I bring a crew and tape it. Hey, it's getting hot out here. Are you sure I can't offer you a drink or a line or something?"

I said, "No, it's a little early in the day for my glass of port. But you can be your wonderfully hospitable self by telling me something."

"Maybe."

"Without mentioning names—I know you don't do that—were any of your regulars people who were outed by John Rutka?"

He stood up now, casually adjusted the organs inside his shorts, and sat down again. "I can answer that, yes," he said. "Two were outed and about ninety-two were scared shitless they were going to be next. For a guy who thought it was so great to be gay, Rutka was some pain in the ass to gay people, that's for sure."

"Did any of your customers seem especially unhinged by being outed, or by the prospect of being outed?"

"I know what you're thinking. When I heard Rutka had been murdered, I wondered the same thing. Who hated him so much or was so afraid of him he'd kill him to shut him up? I don't know. Like I say, every gay person in the closet in Albany hated Rutka's guts. But I never heard anybody say they were actually going to do anything. I'd remember."

"What about this? Have you or any of your staff run into customers who were violent, or seemed capable of great violence?"

"Two," he said without hesitation.

"Can you give me the names?"

"Sure. Fortunately, they're both in prison. Lars Forrester, the Troy bank exec they nailed for embezzlement. And Nelson Lunceford, the state insurance regulator who strangled his valet in the locker room of the Fort Orange Club last year. I had bad reports on both of them."

"They're both still locked up?"

"And will be for a long time. I've kept track of those two."

"What about S&M? Any practitioners? I don't mean the exotic stuff—tarring and feathering and whatnot—but just your plain, old-fashioned, down-home, wholesome types of S&M—hoods and thongs and chains and so forth. Chains especially I'd like to hear about."

He leaned back now, thoughtfully, with his hands behind his head, displaying his exquisite biceps and perfectly tanned armpits. "I can't answer that," Scott said. "For one thing, it's confidential. And anyway, there are too many of them for the information to be of any use to you. There are ten or twelve regulars I can think of

113

right off the top of my head who like the feel of metal."

"Other kinds of metal, too? What do you mean? Pie plates?"

"No, just chains."

"Ah."

"Channel Eight said Rutka was tied up in the house that burned down. Was he bound with chains? Is that why you're asking?"

"Yeah."

"I'll have to think about that—think about different people. You know, Strachey, anybody can go into a hardware store and buy as many feet of chain as they want and have it cut into lengths or anything. I've done it myself. Chains are not just something people use for sex."

"I suppose that's true. What about this?" I said. "I've got three sets of initials. I think they belong to people who know their way around gay Albany. Especially closeted gay Albany. I want to know if these initials mean anything to you."

"I don't know about this. But go ahead."

"J.G."

Now he gave me his profile. *The Thinker.* "Maybe. I can't think. Maybe."

"D.R."

"Mmmm. I don't know. Hmm."

"N.Z."

"Oh—N.Z. Right. Nathan Zenck."

"Nathan Z-E-N-C-K?" He nodded. "Who is Nathan Zenck?"

"He's the assistant manager of the Parmalee Plaza on Wolf Road. He's the night manager, I think."

"Of the hotel or the restaurant?"

"The whole thing. What are these initials? Should I be telling you this?"

114

"Yes, you should, but I can't tell you why. It's confidential."

"I can relate to that."

"Tell me about Nathan."

He sighed, shifted, readjusted his genitals. "He's gay, kind of cute, forty or forty-one, unattached. Travels with the guest accommodations crowd. Likes to party. Nathan's a mover, too. He's been in Albany for two or three years, but I don't imagine he'll want to hang around here. He'll cut out soon. He wants the big time—San Juan or Orlando."

"What else about him?"

"I don't know. What else is there? His sign, his favorite color? What do you mean?"

"I don't know what I mean. Anyway, this is a start. It's been helpful. I appreciate it, Scott."

He leaned forward now across the coffee table that separated us and looked at me and let me catch his scent. He said, "You want me, don't you?"

"Sort of."

"It'll cost you."

I began to laugh, and then Scott S. Scott joined in, so that he wouldn't be left out, and he laughed too.

I stopped by my office, on Central, which I generally avoided in summer since the air conditioner quit early in Reagan's first term, but I wanted to pick up my mail and use the phone. I called Bub Bailey, who told me that the medical examiner had confirmed beyond doubt that the body found in the burned house in Handbag the previous night had been that of John Rutka.

I said, "They're sure?"

"The gunshot wound in the foot, and of course the dental exam. It's the dental that does it. It's as good as fingerprints."

"So that's that."

I half-listened while Bailey went on about the missing files and how critical they were to his investigation. I kept thinking about John Rutka being forced from his house, and chained, and shot, and burned to not much more than ash. Until this moment I hadn't entirely believed it. My reserve of disbelief had salved my conscience over abandoning Rutka when he had pleaded with me not to—even with his scams, maybe he had known he was in real danger—and I had clung at some level to the notion that Rutka was still alive so that I could shake him until his head swam and tell him one more time exactly how little I thought of him. Now I had no hope of any of that and my headache was back, and I deserved it and worse.

I passed on to Bailey what Joel McClurg had told me about the candidate for outing whom Rutka had confessed to being deeply afraid of, but I said I didn't know anything about the files. He muttered something and we both hung up. I found some aspirin in the back of my top desk drawer. The stamp on the back of the container said, "Use before Dec. 1979," so I took three.

15

Nathan Zenck had a telephone listing at an address on Old Tyme Lane in Guilderland. I reached his machine but left no message. I picked up a sub and ate it in the car on the way out to Handbag, where I wanted to see how Sandifer was holding up.

His car was gone and the house was locked up. Out back, a sheet of plywood was leaning against the porch and an assortment of new boards was stacked nearby, along with a roll of screen. Somebody had already started preparations for repairing the fire damage.

On Broad Street I passed the Rutka hardware store, turned around, and pulled into the lot. The place looked prosperous. A big area of the parking lot had been fenced off for a lawn-and-garden department, and the big fleet of red lawn mowers on display looked formidable enough to clip Argentina down to the roots.

Inside, past the appliances department, I asked a clerk, "Is Ann Rutka around? Or is that not her name?"

"She's using Rutka again. Ann's up back." He pointed. Wooden steps led up to a long platform that overlooked the entire store. There was no wall with a one-way glass to spy through and spot shoplifters, just a low railing and a row of desks stacked with catalogs and invoices. Maybe a hardware store was too wholesome a place for shoplifting to occur in. Or maybe shoplifters believed that if they were caught stealing from a hardware store the owner would kill them. It felt like a complex atmosphere to be in.

A woman behind a pile of invoices at the desk nearest me pointed to the farthest desk on the deck, separated from the others by a modest fence of low bookcases filled with parts catalogs.

"Ann Rutka?"

She looked up from a cluttered desk and peered at me with dark eyes from under a heap of ringlets. Rutka's sister was as handsome and well put together as John had been, and she dressed as casually, except her T-shirt wasn't from Queer Nation but bore the logo of a manufacturer of electrical pumps.

"I'm Donald Strachey. I knew your brother and wanted to tell you how sorry I am."

"Thanks." She looked skeptical and didn't put her pencil down. "The funeral's Saturday at nine-thirty at St. Michael's. You're welcome to come." She had a musically rumbly voice that poured out like gravel on the move.

"I'd like to," I said.

She looked at me, waiting.

"I'd also like to give you something," I said, and took out the five-hundred-dollar check Rutka had written as a retainer when he hired me to protect him.

"What's this?"

"I'm a private investigator and John had hired me as a security consultant. This was the retainer he paid me, but I quit after only a few hours. I thought you might want

118

this back for whoever has to straighten out John's finances. Or should I be giving it to Eddie Sandifer?"

She put the pencil down but didn't move otherwise. "No, I'll take it. I'm the executrix, it turns out. Can I ask why you only worked for John for a few hours?"

"Well, I think that has to be between him and me."

"Don't bullshit me, please. I get enough of that. You couldn't put up with him, could you?"

I shrugged. "No."

"Sit down. Do you have a minute?" She motioned me to a tubular chair with a cracked seat.

"Sure."

She flicked a Chesterfield out of a pack and lit it. "What do you mean, he hired you as a security consultant? Do you mean bodyguard?"

"Something like that. He said he wanted protection."

She looked at the date on the check. "John hired you yesterday, and you quit yesterday, and somebody killed him last night. You really are up to your ass in this, aren't you—how do you say your name?"

"STRAY-chee, Don. As in 'Lytton.' Great-uncle Lyt."

She shot smoke back over her shoulder to the air conditioner that rattled in the window frame. "So what are you doing here? Are you feeling guilty? You could have mailed me the check."

"I'm feeling partly responsible."

"I'm not a priest and I can't tell you that you'll be forgiven, Don. But you said that you quit because you couldn't put up with my brother. I believe it. John drove people apeshit. Did he lie to you?"

"Yes, it's my belief that he did."

"Oh, that's your belief, huh? Listen, nobody in Handbag ever believed a word John said. Nobody in Handbag who knew my brother ever trusted him any farther than they could toss him. You just happened to catch on fast. Good for you. Don't feel guilty."

"I guess you and your brother weren't close."

She snorted smoke and her breasts bobbed twice under the sump-pump T-shirt. "We put up with each other. For Mom and Dad's sake. That's why I don't understand something. If John trusted you, maybe you know enough to clear something up for me. How well do you know Eddie?"

"Not well. I'm getting to know him."

"They weren't breaking up, were they? My brother and Eddie?"

"That wasn't my impression. Why?"

She shook her mountains of curls. "Eddie brought me a copy of John's will. Eddie just found it this morning. I checked with our lawyer, Dave Rizzuto, who was about to call me anyway, and he says it's a good will. It was written and filed last month, and John left almost everything to me. To me—the house and his half of the business. All Eddie got was the cash John had on hand and his dirty socks. That's weird."

"Was Eddie upset?"

"I think he was. He seemed surprised, and I think hurt. There's three or four K in John's bank account Eddie will get, but it's the business that's worth real bucks, and of course the house. I'm glad to have it, I'll tell you. My divorce was final in June and I've got three kids who'll all be in college at the same time in a couple of years. But I can't figure out why me if they were still boyfriends. Eddie has been John's real family practically since he's been an adult. Eddie and the activists. So if John trusted you, maybe you know what's going on. John didn't trust too many people. Are you gay?"

"Yes, I am."

"Are you out?"

120

"Sure."

"Well, that would help. I don't think John trusted any straight people—'breeders,' he called us—and the people who really set him off were gay people who pretended they weren't."

"I'm aware of that. As is much of the northeastern United States."

"You might be surprised to know," she said, "that John's campaign to drag gay people out of the closet didn't bother me at all. I can't stand phonies either. We are what we are. Pete, my ex, wasn't too crazy about John going around yelling about queers-this and faggots-that. 'How can he use those words?' Pete'd say. 'If he caught me calling a queer a queer, he'd go apeshit.' Pete missed the point. Pete always missed the point. But John's carrying on was all right with me.

"One of the things I'm really sorry about was that we were never close enough for me to tell him how proud I was of the way he went off to nursing school and pulled his shit together. You'd never believe what a fuckup John was as a teenager. I'm six years older and I was away at school and missed the worst of it, but I heard the stories. And then he went ahead and turned out okay—for John. I sure wish I had the chance to tell my dickhead little brother how I felt about him."

"Maybe he knew," I said. "And he was telling you he knew by leaving you the family house and his half of the business, and he was telling you that he was still part of the Rutka family."

She jabbed out her Chesterfield in a filthy dish full of butts and gave me a look. "You must watch too much television, Donald, and you've gone a little soft in the head. The Rutka family hasn't been a family for a long, long time. I don't even know why John stayed on after Mom and Dad died. There was nothing for him in Handbag. He and I hardly even spoke to each other. I'd tell him changes I was making in the business, but he wasn't really interested. He just wanted his share of the profits. He never said boo to my kids and not much more to me. No, it wasn't family that kept John in Handbag. I don't know why he stayed. It's a total mystery to me."

She fired up another Chesterfield and saw me watching her take a deep drag. "I know," she said, "I know. Soon."

I drove over to the Rutka house and found Eddie Sandifer out back prying up charred boards from the back porch.

"I talked to the chief," he said. "I told him I thought John sent his files to Utica for safekeeping."

"Utica? I thought we decided on Rochester."

"I changed it to Utica because I don't really know anybody there and I don't think John did either."

"Did Bailey seem to buy it?"

"I doubt it. But what's he going to do, beat the truth out of me with a rubber hose? This is Handbag." He ripped up another floorboard and flung it onto the heap out in the yard.

"I hate to do this to a decent guy like Bub Bailey," I said. "But this is the way it has to be for now."

"Hey, I'm cool."

Given the company he'd kept for a decade, I supposed he was. "I think I may have found who one of the sets of initials in the payout ledger belongs to. Have you ever heard of a Nathan Zenck?"

"What's he? No."

"He's a hotel manager in Colonie."

"Never heard of him." He was ripping away at another board that kept splintering and leaving jagged shreds of itself behind.

"I met John's sister," I said. "She told me you'd been by the store."

Sandifer stood up now and wiped the sweat off his face with the side of his arm. He stood there looking as if he was about to speak but was afraid of whatever might come out.

I said, "Ann told me about the will."

Now his shoulders began to shake.

"She was surprised," I said. "And she said you were surprised too, and hurt."

Tears rolled down his face. "Why did John do that?"

I shrugged lamely. "You knew how strange he could be."

Sandifer said, "I don't need the money—it's not that. I can work. But I was like his family. I was more like his family than his real family was. He told me that once. It was hard for him, but he told me. So why did he stiff me?"

"You two hadn't been having any problems?"

"No, I don't think so. No, no, a long time ago. But lately—we loved each other and we thought we'd always be together. So why? Why did he do it?"

I was as stumped as Sandifer, and mad at Rutka all over again. "Well, he left you some money, right?"

"Yes. Several thousand dollars. I'm grateful. I'll be able to use it. I'll have to find a place to live."

We looked at each other, but we'd both run out of words. Again I wanted Rutka to come back from the dead so that I could grab him and force him to answer a list of questions that kept getting longer and longer.

16

I spent three hours back at the house, poring over Rutka's files. I made notes, then compared them and rearranged them, and memorized the data as well as I could. When Timmy got home, I told him I'd have to postpone dinner again and would see him later at the hospital.

At six I drove out to Wolf Road in Colonie.

"I'd like to speak to Mr. Parmalee, please. Could you tell me where his office is?"

The desk clerk at the Parmalee Plaza gave me a chilly once-over and said, "There isn't any Mr. Parmalee. This hotel is owned by the Zantek Corporation and they just call it the Parmalee Plaza."

"How come?"

"I really couldn't tell you that."

"In that case, I'll speak to Mr. Nathan Zenck. I understand he's the night manager."

"Is Mr. Zenck expecting you, sir?"

"No, but he shouldn't be surprised to see me show up."

"Your name, please?"

"Donald Strachey."

"And what is it that you would like to speak to Mr. Zenck about?"

"I'm trying to find out—and maybe he could help me—just who the hell is Parmalee?"

He glared, the telephone receiver he was clutching poised in midair. "I don't know whether I can bother Mr. Zenck with a question like that."

"All right, forget Parmalee. Tell Mr. Zenck I'm an associate of John Rutka and I've got some questions concerning John Rutka's death."

This loosened him up. He blinked several times. "Are you with the police?"

"Were any police officers associates of John Rutka?"

"What?"

"I said I was an associate of John Rutka, and you asked me if I was with the police. You were the one who made the connection. How come?"

"No, I— That's not what I meant. I'll call Mr. Zenck." He picked up the receiver and dialed and waited. "Nathan, a Donald Strachey is here to talk to you about John Rutka, he says." He listened for a quarter of a minute, then hung up. "I'm sorry, but Mr. Zenck doesn't know anyone by that name and he's in conference just now. He says perhaps you can write him a letter. Do you have our mailing address?"

I sighed. "Get him back on the line," I said, "and ask him how would he like it if I called up the Zantek Corporation and got Zantek himself on the line and told him that the night manager of his overpriced, overdecorated new hotel in Colonie, New York, out by the Albany airport, was a scumbag, greedy-ass Peeping Tom, and I had the financial records of a murdered man to prove it? Bother him in conference with that and see what happens."

He looked as if he might put in for an immediate

transfer to some remote, undesirable dead end of an outpost such as, say, Albany, New York, except, ha ha, he was already there. He dialed again.

"I think you'd better talk to Mr. Donald Strachey." He hung up. "Mr. Zenck will be right out."

"Thank you."

Like the desk clerk, Zenck was svelte and silky and meticulously mustachioed, and a little blurry, as if he'd been severely airbrushed. Twenty years earlier this effect could only be achieved on photographs but now it was being done on actual human beings, though I didn't know how.

"Mr. Strachey?"

"I am he."

"Nice to see you." He beamed. "Why don't we step into my office?"

"Let's step."

I followed him down the corridor and past an unmarked door, which he closed behind us. Zenck's spacious-enough digs included a desk with a marble top and a computer terminal off to one side, two leather couches, a small bar, and a couple of rust-colored rectangles in silver frames placed on the otherwise bare walls as if they were family portraits. Also among the furnishings was a series of small-screen video monitors mounted on racks next to Zenck's desk. One showed the spot at the front desk where I had recently been standing. Another showed a panning shot of the restaurant, which at six-fifteen was nearly filled. A third shot swept the hotel lobby and a fourth the murky bar.

A fifth screen was blank, and I said to Zenck, "What do you look at on that one, guests in the privacy of their rooms?"

"Won't you sit down?" he said.

I plopped onto one couch and he stood by the other.

"Would you care for a drink?"

"Unh-unh."

He sat down, adjusted his jacket, and said, "Did you say you were a friend of John Rutka's? That's the man who was murdered, isn't it?" He gave me a concerned look.

I said, "John Rutka's financial records show that he made sizeable monthly cash payments to you in return for reports on who among your paying guests was fucking whom. I'm investigating Rutka's death and want to ask you some things about your sideline racket. First off—"

"Whoa, whoa, whoa," he said, shaking his head and grinning. "I think you have me mixed up with someone else—Don, is it?"

"Donald Strachey. I'm a private investigator in Albany. I worked for John Rutka and have had access to his records. You're in there. All over the place—Nate, is it?"

"Nathan. But you really must have me—"

"Well, Nathan, it's all down in black and white. Amounts, dates the cash was delivered, and information on your guests' activities that's noted as coming from you and could only have come from one source."

He looked at me beadily. "That's a lie. Those are lies. Is there anything in those records in my handwriting?"

"No, but the stuff obviously came from you. Anybody going through it can see that. Any jury would be convinced."

He tried to cover up the shudder that went through him, but couldn't. "Oh, God."

I said, "Your front-desk man struck me as a man who would not hold up well under cross-examination in a courtroom. And of course if the cops came out here with a flying squad and interrogated every desk clerk and chambermaid and busboy and bartender who was

slipped ten bucks for tipping you off on a local person-
age apparently involved in some same-sex conjoining on
the hotel premises, a certain number of them would be
sure to own up. It's mere statistical probability. But—
lucky for you—the cops haven't seen those records yet,
and they may never. That depends."

"Depends on what?" he croaked.

"On whether I'm satisfied with the quality of the information you give me."

"You'd go to the police?"

"Sure."

"This is blackmail. This is fucking blackmail!"

The mind reeled. "Nathan, are you raising moral objec-
tions to my exposure of your practice of selling information on people's private sexual activities to a man who
then published the information in the newspapers? Are
you presuming to question me on ethical grounds?"

He twitched once but otherwise sat looking glum. "It
was just dish," he finally said. "I don't see why you don't
get it. I know about you, Strachey, and I know you're
gay, and I don't see where you get off acting so fucking
holier-than-thou. Don't tell me you never dished anybody."

" 'Dished'? You made thirty-two hundred dollars tax-
free this year providing a lunatic with information on
who went into which hotel room with whom, and sometimes what kind of stains were left on the sheets, and
condoms in the wastebaskets, and every other piece of
crud you could come up with, and you call that 'dish'?"

"Yes. I do. And maybe if you'd lighten up a little,
Strachey, you would too. I'm just being gay. I don't know
what the fuck *you're* trying to be. Gay people have been
doing each other forever, and gay people will be doing
each other until the end of time. That's just a part of being
gay, and maybe it's about time people like you faced it

128

and quit trying to pretend you're something you're not!"

I wished Rutka were there to hear those words. Here was the kind of classic gay self-loathing—"internalized homophobia"—that John Rutka had despised and fought against with every atom of his being, and it turned out to be coming from a man who had played a critical part in making Rutka's antihomophobia campaign possible. It was as if enlightened gay thought existed not on a spectrum but in a circle, and the evilest underside of the circle was where, facing each other from opposite directions, Nathan Zenck and John Rutka met. One outed gay people because he loved them, ostensibly, and one because he hated them, and it all amounted to the same thing: oceans of pain and conflict and nothing to show for it.

I said, "Either you answer my questions to my satisfaction, or I will go to both the cops and the Zantek Corporation with everything I've got. You choose, Nathan. How's that for gay people doing each other till the end of time? Of course, I haven't got till the end of time. I'm going to give you about twenty minutes."

"I'll get you for this."

"You will? How?"

"I'll blacken your name from Niskayuna to Selkirk."

"No, please."

"I mean it."

I felt as if I'd been caught in a time warp. Next he'd be addressing me as "Bitch." I said, "I'll just have to live with the horror of it all."

"You laugh about it now. But you wait."

I'd had enough. "Just shut up and answer my questions, you pitiful anachronism, or I swear I'll ruin your life."

That did it. He clamped his mouth shut and sat there stewing in his silk suit. I felt silly and ashamed meeting

Zenck on his own terms, but he didn't know that, so I went ahead and did what I had gone there to do.

"When you first heard that John Rutka had been killed," I said, "who did you think of first? Who did you think might have done it?"

He had probably been expecting something a little more pointed and specific than this, and he appeared to relax somewhat. "I really have no idea who killed John. It could have been dozens of people. How would I know? I was just shocked."

"That's not what my question was. Who did you think it might have been? What went through your mind?"

"Well, Bruno Slinger, naturally. I know his balls went into orbit when John outed him. You just don't fuck around with Miss Bruno, Miss Queen of the New York State Senate."

"Do you know Slinger?"

"Doesn't every cute guy in Albany under the age of a hundred and six know Miss Bruno? I can't imagine he hasn't popped your cork."

"Did you ever hear him threaten Rutka?"

"Not personally, I didn't. But I get all the best dirt."

"What did you hear?"

"Just that Bruno said people like Rutka should be exterminated like roaches. I can't remember who told me exactly, but I heard it more than once."

A phone next to Zenck rang once and he picked it up. "Yes?" He listened. "Well, you'll just have to handle it. I do not wish to be disturbed." He listened again. "We are *not*. Winston, *you* handle it." He slammed the receiver down.

"Who else did you think of," I said, "when you heard John had been killed? Bruno and who else?"

"Oh, I don't know. Ronnie Linkletter. He was going around saying John should be boiled in oil. Stuff like that. Naturally, I'd think of dear Ronnie."

130

"Were either Slinger or Linkletter into S&M at all? Tying people up with chains or whatever?"

"I never heard that. I don't know. They never left any chains here. I'd have heard about that."

"And sold the information to John Rutka?"

"Why not? He was buying, and why shouldn't I sell him what he wanted if I had it? That's what makes the world go 'round."

It was becoming apparent that there wasn't anything Zenck knew that might be useful that wasn't already in Rutka's files, because Zenck had sold the dirt to Rutka, who put it there.

I said, "Who's the All-American Asshole Mega-Hypocrite?"

"The what?"

"Did Rutka ever mention a mega-hypocrite—somebody who was gay and closeted and deserved more than anybody else to be outed? Somebody who was sickeningly or even dangerously hypocritical?"

This involved a moral consideration that might simply have been outside Zenck's ken. He looked baffled. "I wouldn't know about that. Miss Bruno, maybe. After the job she did on that law some gay people were in favor of against beating up fags and what have you. I wouldn't really know who else it could be." He glanced at his watch. "You know, Strachey, delicious as it is sitting here being whipped with your rubber hose, I do have other responsibilities to attend to. Could we wrap this up in about, say, half a sec?"

"No, we can't. Where were you last night between six and nine, Nathan?"

He simpered. "Right here, honey-chile. The same place I am every night Monday through Friday from six P.M. to two A.M. Now, I think I am going to have to ask you to excuse me, Donald. People are starting to wonder what we're doing in here." He started to stand up.

131

"Sit, Nathan. I'm not finished."

He hesitated, got into a sulk, and sat.

"Who else performed this sleazy snooping service for Rutka besides you?"

He sniffed. "Just Jay, that I know of. Jay Gladu. Isn't he in the records too?"

Jay Gladu—JG. "Just answer my questions, please. Who else?"

"He's the only one I know about. I just happen to know Jay because he's in the hospitality and guest-accommodations business too. If you want to call it that."

"He's where—at the Sheraton?"

This got a snicker. "You must have him mixed up with someone else. Jay runs a hot-sheet motel on Central Avenue, the Fountain of Eden. Who's at the Sheraton? John never mentioned that he had a contact there."

"I'll ask the questions, Nathan, and you'll answer them. Whose initials are the letters DR?"

He sniffed and thought. "DR?"

"DR, yes."

"Zantek has a hotel in the D.R.—the Dominican Republic. It's a full resort and convention facility, and we had a sales meeting down there two years ago, the Surf 'n' Smurf. That's the only D.R. I know of."

"Zantek actually has a hotel that's called the Surf 'n' Smurf?"

"It's a family resort. If you want fast-lane resort life, the Surf 'n' Smurf is not for you."

"I suppose not."

It seemed unlikely that John Rutka had been making cash disbursements to the Dominican Republic, but that was the only D.R. Zenck seemed to know. Maybe Jay Gladu would know who or what D.R. was.

I said, "Nathan, I'm going to get up and leave now and you are going to utter a deep sigh of relief. I'm not going to notify the police or the Zantek Corporation of your sleazy practices—not, that is, unless I return for additional information and you refuse to give me what I want. In that case, I'll destroy you. Also, if I ever learn that you are once again spying on any of your guests, as you did for John Rutka, I will do everything within my power to smash your career in hospitality and guest accommodations to little tiny bits and pieces. You'll be an assistant towel boy by the pool at the Surf 'n' Smurf until you're collecting Social Security. Do you understand what I'm saying?"

He glowered up at me. *Now* he's going to call me a bitch, I thought, but the moment passed and he didn't. He stood up, opened the door to the corridor, and said, "Good *night!*"

"Don't forget my warning, you weasel," I said, and shoved the door shut in his face. The shouted word was just barely audible through the thick door, but I could make it out.

17

I phoned Sandifer from the Parmalee Plaza lobby and asked him if he would like to spend the night at our place again. He said no, a friend from New York had come up; the two of them would stay at the house in Handbag and he would be okay. He sounded less desperate than he had been earlier in the day, and I was relieved to hear it.

Jay Gladu's number was unlisted. I phoned the Fountain of Eden on Route 5 between Albany and Schenectady. The desk clerk wouldn't tell me Gladu's home phone number but said I could leave a message, which I declined to do. I asked when Gladu was likely to show up in person and was told between nine and ten in the morning. This was probably to pick up the overnight receipts.

I reached Bub Bailey at his office in Handbag. He said, "How's your investigation going, Mr. Strachey?"

" 'Investigation' is too grand a word for it, Chief, but I'm doing what little asking around I can."

"That's nice of you. Have you been able to pick up anything yet?"

"Nothing to speak of. How about you? I missed the six o'clock news tonight."

"I have had one piece of good luck," Bailey said mildly. "Two of my officers were combing the driveway area of the Rutka house and they came up with something the abductor may have left behind—a piece of a mud flap from his car. It broke off somehow, or was ripped off, and my officers came across it. It's not from Rutka's car, and Edward Sandifer says no other cars have parked in the driveway to his knowledge. Most park at curbside. So this may be our first real break."

"Can you tell what kind of car it came from?"

"Big, probably American, maybe GM or Chrysler. That's as close as we can get. I'm not making news of the mud flap public, and I'm sure you can understand why. The killer would simply replace his damaged flap and we'd be back where we started. And I can't ask every department in the capital district to go crawling around under all the big American cars looking at mud flaps. That wouldn't make me too popular. But I wanted you to know."

"Thank you, Chief."

"One of my officers will be in Albany this evening and if you'd like, he could stick a photocopy of the mud flap slice in your mailbox—just in case."

"That can't hurt. Thanks." I gave him my street address.

"The bad news is," Bailey said, "that the state lab couldn't find any fingerprints on the note left at the fire scene. Whoever wrote it was being very careful. And the only prints on John's wallet were his own. This all fits in with what we already know about the killer—that he seems to be cold-blooded and methodical."

I said, "I guess I'm not surprised. It seems as though you're looking for someone who's been so unhinged by

John's outing campaign that he'll actually kill for revenge, but not so unhinged he wasn't able to go about
it in a businesslike way."

"It would certainly help," Bailey said, "if I could get
hold of those files John kept. Edward Sandifer says they
were sent to Utica for safekeeping but he claims he
doesn't know the name of the person out there who has
them."

"I'm sure he'd give you the name if he had it, Chief.
Eddie wants John's killer caught more than anybody."

"Well, he did give me a list of people who threatened
John, and I'm piecing together what I can with copies of
Cityscape and *Queerscreed* and through interviews. Plus,
I'm picking up the odd unsolicited tip here and there.
I've had two anonymous phone calls, for instance, telling
me I'd better check out this Bruno Slinger and find out
where he was last night at the time of the abduction and
murder. I drove down to the capitol this afternoon and
Mr. Slinger wasn't too happy to see me. He had the gall
to tell me that he had an alibi for yesterday evening but
it was none of my business what it was and I'd just have
to take his word for it that he had nothing to do with the
murder."

"That sounds like Bruno. He works for a very powerful
man, and he sees himself as a kind of prince."

"Since I have no other evidence beyond the anonymous calls and the unsubstantiated allegation that Mr.
Slinger threatened John several months ago," Bailey said,
"there's nothing more I can do with him at this point. We
discreetly located and checked the mud flap on his car,
and the mud flap section found at the Rutka house was
not Mr. Slinger's. But if I can come up with anything else
on him at all, I'll see what I can do to get him in and
depose him. You wouldn't have any information on Mr.
Slinger that you're holding back, would you, Mr. Strachey?"

"Chief, I wish I did. I mean, not that I'd hold it back. I just wish I knew anything that could help out, and that I could pass along."

A silence. This guy had my number—had had it for probably twenty-four hours.

I said, "Anyway, I'll keep in touch."

"I'm counting on that," he said, and it began to dawn on me that that was exactly what he was doing, counting on me.

I phoned the house and Timmy was out—probably, I figured, at Albany Med. I punched in the code and listened to the single message that had been left on my machine. A male voice I did not recognize, and that I was reasonably certain I had never heard, said, "If you want to find out who killed John Rutka, ask Bruno Slinger who he was with last night." Click. That was all.

At first I was irritated. I was weary of all the secrecy and duplicity and dreary bitchery and I was also fed up with people like Nathan Zenck who seemed to *deserve* all the secrecy and duplicity and dreary bitchery. And my first impulse was to dismiss the call, as well as the anonymous calls Bub Bailey had received, as useless backstabbing—one or more of Bruno Slinger's hundreds of enemies setting him up to be harassed and humiliated in public.

Then it occurred to me, why was I receiving an anonymous call? Word could not have spread far that I was working on the case and it seemed likely that only truly knowledgeable people would know that I was the man to call with a hot tip.

Plus, something about the caller's words made me wonder. He hadn't said, "Slinger did it—I saw him," or "Slinger's the killer—he'll confess under torture." The caller had said, "If you want to find out who killed John Rutka, ask Bruno Slinger who he was with last night." As if Slinger hadn't done it, but somehow he could provide

137

the key to who had done it by telling me who he'd been with while the murder was taking place. Slinger wasn't the key, but his alibi was.

Or maybe this was just more duplicity. I'd have to find out.

Slinger was unlisted in the Albany phone book, though I knew where he lived on Chestnut Street, around the corner from our place on Crow. I phoned a friend of Timmy's in the legislature who I knew would have Slinger's home number, and he gave it to me on the condition that I not mention where I'd gotten it. I dialed.

"Yes?"

"Don Strachey, Bruno. I'm a private investigator and I'm doing some work for someone on the John Rutka case. I have Rutka's files. You're in there. We should talk."

A pause. Then: "You're scum."

"For the time being, I am. But these things work themselves out ethically in the end, I'm told. Could I drop by?"

"No, you could not. I'm on my way out. What do you want from me?"

"Just to talk and to ask a couple of questions, and maybe to reassure you regarding the ultimate disposition of Rutka's files."

"Are you going to demand money?"

"Would you pay it if I did?"

"Don't be ridiculous."

"So, now that neither of us feels so threatened by the other, what's a good time for me to drop by? I live in your neighborhood and I stay up late. Around eleven?"

"I know exactly who you are and I know exactly where you live. Do you mean eleven o'clock tonight?"

"If a passerby spotted a known homosexual like me knocking at your door, I'd just tip my hat and say I was a neighbor dropping by to borrow a cup of sulphuric acid."

138

"Don't get funny with me. It's not a good idea. All right, eleven o'clock." He hung up.

On my way out of the Parmalee Plaza, the desk clerk shrank back when I glowered at him menacingly.

"I feel like J. Edgar Hoover," I told Timmy in the corridor outside room F-5912. "I lie to people, I bully and threaten and manipulate people, I invade their privacy—and all for some higher cause." I had just given him a rundown on the day's events.

"Hoover never did anything for a higher cause. He was an evil psychopath, nothing more."

"Oh, thank you. Now I feel better."

"No, I know why you're doing it. To solve the murder and then destroy the files. But you don't have to use Hoover's methods—or John Rutka's."

"But these are the kind of people it turns out I'm dealing with, evil Hoovers and screwed-up Rutkas. The Hoovers are so repulsive I'm almost enjoying hoisting them on their own petards."

He said, "I think you might even be starting to look a little like Hoover. You should get some rest—and food. Have you not eaten again?"

"I'll agree not to look like Hoover if you agree not to look like Clyde."

"I promise not to for the next ten years or so. After that—hey."

"No, I haven't eaten," I said. "I'm going over to Bruno Slinger's after I leave here, so I could use some coffee and a Mars bar or whatever people dine on around here after the cafeteria closes. Where can I pick something up?"

"Why don't you go in and see Mike and Stu and I'll scrounge up what I can?"

"Thanks. I'll provide you with some unsatisfying, undernourishing repast someday."

"I'm sure you will."

Timmy went down the corridor after a phalanx of priests who'd just come out of Bishop McFee's room and I went into room F-5912 past the skeletal comatose man nobody paid any attention to. Stu Meserole lay amidst the machinery, which looked like some droll array of bleeping and gurgling nonsensical equipment from one of the Ealing comedies of the early fifties.

Stu had discovered the Ealing gems in a video store during his last year of consciousness and they had filled him with delight. Timmy and I were with him when Stu watched *The Lavender Hill Mob* and *The Ladykillers* and *The Man in the White Suit* for the second or third time. Now I half expected a demented-looking Alec Guinness to rise up from behind Stu's machinery wielding a smoking beaker that would turn out to contain a cure.

But he didn't. Rhoda Meserole said, "Hello, Donald. It was good of you to come."

"How is he?"

"Oh, the same. All we can do is pray."

Al Meserole was inexplicably missing, freeing up the most comfortable chair for Rhoda. Mike was in his customary seat, and stood up when I came in. He signaled for me to step outside the room, which I did after briefly grasping Stu's limp hand.

"Al's gone," Mike whispered. "He went back to work."

"But Rhoda's still here all the time?"

"Yes, but she's letting down her guard. The woman is human, after all. She goes to the john, she goes to the cafeteria. Sometimes she's gone for half an hour at a time. I could do it. All I need is the drug. You're going to get something for me, aren't you?"

"Yes."

"When?"

"What did the doctor say today?"

"The same as yesterday. I asked him again just to be

certain. The part of Stu's brain that made him human doesn't exist anymore. Stu is dead. It's a travesty what's going on in that room. When can you get me something? I'll pay you whatever it costs."

"I'll have to call someone in New York. You might have to go down and pick it up."

"I can't."

"Why?"

"Rhoda would be suspicious. When I got back, she'd never leave Stu out of her sight."

"I'm kind of tied up around here. And Timmy—he'll have to be told, but he won't want to be involved. He'll accept it, but he won't be able to bring himself to participate. I can get it Fed-Exed up, I guess."

"When can you get it?"

"I'll call New York tonight and let you know tomorrow."

"Don't put it off, okay?"

"I won't."

He squeezed my hand and went back into the room.

When Timmy came back, he said, "Don't tell me. I do understand, but don't tell me."

"I don't know what you're talking about," I said, and we left it at that.

18

"Where's the file?" Slinger said, gaping at my empty-handedness. "You didn't bring it with you?"

" 'It'?"

"You said you had the file Rutka kept on me. Do you mean to say you didn't bring it?"

I was seated on a settee across from Slinger in the living room of his Chestnut Street townhouse with the air conditioner on high and a gas fire blazing symmetrically in the fireplace. The portrait hanging above the mantel was of the Republican leader of the state senate, and on a sideboard there were signed photos in silver frames of, among others, Roy Cohn, Barbara Walters, and Adnan Khashoggi.

Slinger leaned toward me, looking edgy and vaguely predatory, and it was hard to resist the urge to back away. He was a big man and it was plain that under his dressing gown he had the massive chest and shoulders of someone who worked out an hour or two a day. He had a granite face with angry gray eyes, and wore a pompadoured hairpiece worthy of a CNN anchor.

Slinger suddenly pulled something from the pocket of

his gown and flipped it onto the mahogany coffee table between us.

"What have we here, Bruno?"

"Count it."

"That won't be necessary."

"It's five thousand dollars. Take it. I'll trust you to walk home and bring back the file."

"The file is staying where it is, but that's beside the point."

He looked at me and made no move to take back the wad of cash wrapped with a rubber band. "I suppose you want me to suck your dick," he said. "Is that what this is all about? You want me to come over there and get down on my knees and suck your cock and lick your balls."

"Why did you work so hard to kill the hate-crimes bill?" I said.

He fell back now and snorted once. "I don't believe this. You call me up and threaten me with Rutka's god-damn files and then when I try to play your game the way you want it played, you back off. What's with you anyway, Strachey? What do you want?"

I said, "It's true, I did introduce the subject of the files in hopes of getting your cooperation, Bruno. But I don't want your money, and God knows I don't want you slobbering on any part of me. I just want you to answer two questions and then we can talk about the files. The first question is—I repeat—why did you work so hard to kill the hate-crimes bill?"

He shifted his gown and crossed his legs huffily. "It's a waste of time."

"The bill?"

"People who beat up queers are people who are going to beat up queers. They don't give a good goddamn what the law says."

"Convict a few of them and put their pictures on the

front of the *Post* being led off in chains," I said, "and word will get around. Some of them who'd otherwise do it will think twice. It'd make a difference, just like the federal civil-rights laws helped end lynching in the South."

"Honey, you live in a dream world," he said, sniffing. "Anyway, if a couple of stupid queens go swishing around down by the docks at three in the morning, maybe they're asking for trouble."

"What if they're swishing around at Seventh and Bleecker at eleven-thirty? Or Third and St. Mark's Place at ten to ten? Are you suggesting that there should be times and places when queer-bashing is restricted and times and places when it's not? How about alternate-side-of-the-street queer-bashing, and violators will have their bricks and lead pipes towed away? You're a dealmaker, Bruno. How's that for a compromise?"

He sighed deeply. "You know goddamn well why I worked against the legislation, Strachey. The man I work for hates fags. The senator believes homosexuality is an abomination and homosexuals are abominable and they deserve whatever they get."

"Whatever 'they' get?"

"All right. We."

"Do you share the senator's views, Bruno?"

He reddened and for a long moment said nothing. Then: "I do what everybody does who can get away with it. I get on top and I stay there through any means at my disposal. If you're not doing that, my self-righteous friend, it is because you are weak."

I thought, Oh, hell, he's one of those. Arguing with one was like climbing a greased pole, except less intellectually rewarding.

I said, "Does the senator actually believe that you're not gay, that Rutka's column was a smear campaign by the Democratic minority in the senate?"

144

He chuckled. "Yes."

"Well, if you don't answer my next question, Bruno, I'm going to march into the senator's office the first time you're not there to guard the door, and I'm going to dump John Rutka's entire dossier on you onto the senator's desk—notes, memos, diaries, audiotapes, video-tapes—a veritable Library of Congress of your sexual misadventuring. A lurid mixed-media cavalcade featuring Bruno Slinger and a variety of chaps in their birthday suits, wienies agog. What would you think of that?"

"I would consider it the act of a desperate scumbag. Are you saying there are actual tapes? I find that hard to believe."

"Remember Kevin?" I made this up.

"Oh, God."

"You didn't know you were being taped?" I made this up too. There were no audio- or videotapes of anyone in any of Rutka's files.

"I can't remember who would have— Oh, God."

I said, "Tell me who you were with last night."

"That's the other question?"

"That's it. Answer it and then we can talk about the disposition of your file."

He looked more confident now. "The Handbag police chief came into my office today—just walked right in unannounced. If he had stayed a second longer, I would have had to ask the Capitol Police to remove him. The man apparently suspects me of John Rutka's murder. Can you imagine?"

"Of course I can imagine. Practically everybody who knows you can. When Rutka outed you in *Cityscape,* you told people you were going to rip his balls off. You probably wouldn't even think of it as murder, just real-politik. That's what people think. Did you do it?"

Without batting an eyelash, Slinger said, "John Rutka deserved what he got. He was a danger to society who

145

deserved to be removed from it one way or another. I laughed when I heard he was dead. I was *dee*-lighted. But of course I had nothing to do with it. I'm not stupid. Too many people would want to pin it on me and I'm far too intelligent to make myself vulnerable by actually committing the noble but unfortunately unlawful deed. No, I did not kill John Rutka, and I can prove it."

"How? What's your alibi for last night?"

"I spent the evening with two of Albany's most distinguished citizens. Both of them will vouch for my presence at a small get-together in Colonie from approximately seven P.M. until just before midnight."

"Do these two distinguished citizens have names?"

"Ronnie Linkletter and Scooter Raymond."

Only in the benighted age in which we live could a local TV weatherman and a pretty-boy dim-bulb anchor on the six o'clock news be described by anyone, even a man with a mind as warped as Bruno Slinger's, as "distinguished."

Scooter Raymond was a recent arrival in Albany, brought in by Channel Eight to replace the ancient, tightly wound Clem Snodgrass after Snodgrass suffered an on-air stroke that left him repeating the words "Back to you, Flossie—Back to you, Flossie—Back to you, Flossie" twelve or fifteen times before the picture switched to co-anchor Flossie Proctor, a woman normally seen with her head thrown back in inexplicable perpetual ecstasy but who appeared vaguely human for the first time in twenty years the night Clem Snodgrass's neurons began to pop on-camera.

In a line of endeavor where the men are permitted to bear a striking physical resemblance to Joseph Stalin in his tomb but the women are expected to show up every night looking like *The Birth of Venus*, Flossie Proctor was no kid. There were those who speculated that Flos-

146

sie's days were numbered now that she shared the anchor desk with a man who had fewer chins than she. I knew nothing of Scooter Raymond other than what I'd learned from Channel Eight's promos welcoming him to the Hometown Folks news team: that Scooter was "an experienced newsgatherer"—like Harrison Salisbury, it was suggested, except twinklier—and that Scooter had already begun to think of Albany as his hometown, as if this were an acquired trait. The station had announced additionally that "Scooter is his real name," which few doubted.

I asked Slinger, "Who else was in attendance at this get-together besides you and Ronnie and Scooter?"

"No one, actually," he said casually. "It was a combined work and let-down-your-hair session of the type I often initiate with new media people who come to town. I had the opportunity to brief Scooter on some of the ins and outs of the legislature and its personalities, and at the same time I was able to promote some of the senator's thoughts on directions the state should be taking."

"And Ronnie was there to represent the meteorological point of view, or what?"

"He drove," Slinger said, looking bemused. "Scooter needed a ride, and Ronnie drove."

"To where? Where did this informal information-sharing session take place? In public, I hope."

"Public enough," Slinger said, still looking on top of the game. "We met in a suite that I keep reserved for the senator's use at the Parmalee Plaza Hotel. It's convenient to the airport. Executives and officials from the city can fly in and meet the senator and be back at LaGuardia in an hour."

"So the people who can vouch for your whereabouts last night are Ronnie and Scooter and—who else?"

"Several hotel employees saw us arrive and depart—

the desk clerk and the night manager, who both know me, among others. There's no doubt I was out there, Strachey. It's easily verifiable."

"Did you tell the Handbag police chief that's where you were?"

"I most certainly did not."

"Why not?"

"Because he had no legal basis for his harassing me in my place of work. It was a goddamn outrage, is what it was."

"You were outraged, but he has a right to question you and he will likely exercise that right."

"If that mealy-mouthed constable wants to talk to me, he can show me a warrant and I'll notify my attorney and we'll see. He won't obtain a warrant, of course, because no judge will issue one without evidence. That I was once angry at John Rutka and said I was so mad I could kill him is not evidence. People say things like that all the time and it's meaningless in court."

Slinger seemed not to know about the anonymous phone calls Bub Bailey had received pointing at Slinger and the one left on my machine telling me that if I wanted to know who killed John Rutka I should find out who Slinger had been with the night before. If Slinger was telling the truth about spending the evening at the Parmalee Plaza, it seemed likely that someone who worked at the hotel was the mystery caller, though not Zenck or the desk clerk; I would have recognized their voices. The caller, of course, could also have been any-one visiting or staying at the place who had seen Slinger come and go. It could also have been someone else present in the suite whom Slinger had not mentioned.

I said, "Chief Bailey can't make you talk because he hasn't got anything on you. But I do—the files. So, tell me this, Bruno. Who else was in the suite with you and Ronnie and Scooter?"

"No one."

"Did you have sex?"

He grinned hideously.

"The three of you?"

"Scooter watched. He's not gay, he says, but he likes to watch. He loves seeing the weatherman being fucked, he says. At the last place he worked, in Sacramento, he liked to watch the weatherman being fucked."

"I guess this is the result of Reagan-era broadcast deregulation."

"I happen to like fucking slender, angelic-looking young men like Ronnie Linkletter, and Ronnie happens to enjoy being serviced by powerful older men of superior intellect."

"Uh-huh."

"Ronnie's a beauty, isn't he? I consider myself extremely fortunate. I'd been hearing for years that he was a fag but that he was faithful to someone who had won Ronnie's heart with the majesty of his position. Lucky for me, they apparently had some sort of falling-out this summer, and I was able to move in and fill the breach, as it were."

I said, "You don't know who this powerful person was?"

"Ronnie refuses to discuss him, which I appreciate. It means he'll tend to be discreet in what he tells others about me. My motto has always been, If you're going to be indiscreet, be discreet about it. That's why I plan my assignations these days at the Parmalee Plaza. It's gay-run, as you're probably aware, and in return for an occasional remuneration, the night manager will see that his people will keep their mouths shut about who's doing whom out there."

"Right."

"Ronnie used to go to that vomitorium Jay Gladu runs out on Central Avenue, and he tried to get me into it, but

I wouldn't set foot in the place. I do safe sex only, for the most part, and it's unsafe just walking in the door of the Fountain of Eden. Have you ever been out there?"

"Not yet," I said. "Why do you use motels? Couldn't you bring your sex partners here?"

"Do you see those photographs?" Slinger said, growing somber and motioning at the lineup on the sideboard.

"They're quite a bunch."

"One picture is missing. It was stolen by a man I brought here once, and it is irreplaceable. The photograph was given to me when I was very young, and it had on it a warm greeting to me from a very great man. Would you like to know who it was?"

"Yes, who?"

"Henry Pu Yi, the last emperor of China."

"Oh."

"Briefly, we were lovers."

"Were you mentioned in the movie?"

"No."

"Well, then—I guess that made the photo even more important. Your only memento."

"That's why I never bring people I don't trust into my home."

I said, "Do you only have sex with people you don't trust?"

I'd have felt pretty demeaned if somebody had asked me that question, but Slinger just shrugged and said, "It's the best way of knowing what to expect from people," and then he dropped the subject.

"I'm not going to give you your file," I said.

"I'm not surprised."

"But after John Rutka's killer is caught, I'm going to destroy them all."

"Oh? How will I be certain that you've done it? I have no reason to trust you, Strachey."

150

"You'll never know for sure. I'm sorry about that."

"No, you're not. You're not sorry at all."

"Okay, you're right. In your case, Bruno, I'm not sorry at all."

He sneered contentedly.

I left Slinger's house and went out into the clammy night air. The headache I'd had earlier in the day was gone, but now my stomach was churning. It was partly because I'd had only a Mars bar for dinner, but not entirely.

I made my call to New York on behalf of Mike Sciola from the phone in the cubbyhole under the stairs. In the age of AIDS, the murder of friends and lovers dying horribly is an act of mercy so common as to border on respectability—in a saner world United Way would be putting out brochures on the subject—and I had no trouble making the arrangements Mike had asked for.

19

I watched the 8:25 A.M. local-news insert in "Have a Nice Day, USA" on the monitor in the Channel Eight foyer. Troy Pillsbury, the morning anchor, reported on a flaming six-car pileup on the Northway; on Albany judge and Federal Appeals Court nominee "Pincher" Goerlach's approval in Washington by the Senate Judiciary Committee despite protests from liberal groups over his outbursts from the Albany bench directed at "adherents of deviant lifestyles"; and on the previous evening's bon voyage ceremonies at the Albany airport, where Scooter Raymond was seeing off a schoolgirl and her parents, who were carrying the bird with the broken wing to Minnesota.

After the commercial, Ronnie Linkletter came on and he and Pillsbury acted hugely amused with each other for no reason discernible to viewers. Ronnie predicted continued balmy weather, to which Troy replied, "That's the way we like it." They both chuckled at this *mot.*

Linkletter had insisted to me on the phone an hour earlier—when I of course threatened him with blackmail

152

if he refused to see me—that I not come to the station. I said I preferred to meet him there—I wanted to check his mud flaps—and we could have breakfast somewhere else. When I arrived, I didn't know which of the eight cars in the Channel Eight lot was Linkletter's, but none had damaged, missing, or newly replaced mud flaps, so that was that.

At 8:35 Linkletter came out grinning, still delighted, I guessed, with the Shavian wit of his exchanges with Troy Pillsbury. His smile fell away, though, once we were away from the Channel Eight building and inside my car.

"You're a real asshole," he said. "It isn't bad enough that John Rutka practically ruined me. Now you're going to come after me, too, with his fucking file on me." He looked as if he might burst into tears.

"Look, I just used the files to get your attention. Just answer some questions for me, Ronnie, and I promise you that when John Rutka's killer is caught, the files will be trashed. I'll do it myself."

His sweet boy's face with the button nose and round soft eyes got a stricken look and he struggled for control. "What do you mean, get my attention? What are you trying to get me to *tell* you? You *are* blackmailing me!"

"I truly do not want to hurt you, Ronnie, because I know you've been hurt already and you don't need this. Just answer a couple of questions to help me out and that's probably all I'll need from you."

"Probably!"

We had pulled out onto Central Avenue and were headed east in the fuming stop-and-go morning traffic. "What happens next," I said, "all depends on the veracity and the particular nature of your answers. So take care."

"Oh, Jesus."

"The first question is, of course, did you kill John Rutka?"

First he jerked up, as if I'd jabbed him with a pitchfork, and then he began to shake all over. I said, "Does that mean your answer is yes, or no?"

"No! No! Jesus, of course not!"

"You threatened him after he outed you."

Linkletter's slight body writhed in his seat belt. "Well, of course I did. I was fucking out of my *mind*. The man nearly ruined my *life*. All I ever wanted was to be in the media, and that asshole almost blew my career right out of the water. Sporkin Communications has let me know—indirectly of course—that when my contract is up next year it might be nice if I had something lined up in Montana or some other diddly-doo minor market. John Rutka was shit. I'm sorry somebody killed him, but he was shit and he deserved to die. I don't mean actually die, but you know what I mean."

I said, "I agree that Rutka did things to people that were all wrong and you were one of those people."

"Then why are you harassing me too?"

"So that I can find out who killed John Rutka and then get rid of the bloody files. Get it?"

"Oh, sure." He looked unimpressed.

"So. Where were you Wednesday night, Ronnie?"

"When Rutka was killed?"

"Yes. Between, say, seven and ten?"

"At a meeting. At the Parmalee Plaza Hotel."

"And Scooter Raymond watched, right?"

That got him with the pitchfork again and he jerked up and then he jerked down. Here I was, taking out my pent-up disgust with the monumental inanity of local television news on this unlucky twerp. I resolved to be more objective with Linkletter from that moment on.

"How do you know about that?" he moaned.

"That wasn't fair, I admit, but I'm trying to evaluate your trustworthiness."

154

"Maybe somebody should evaluate *yours.*"

He had me there. I pulled off Central into the parking lot of Albany's premier Long Island–style, Athenian-glitz diner and parked at the deserted far end of the lot.

I said, "I talked to Bruno Slinger last night."

"Oh. I guess I'm his alibi and he's mine. And Scooter's too."

"Bruno thinks you're wonderful."

Now some of the tension went out of him and he let loose with a wan little grin. "I know. I think *he's* wonderful."

I said, "Even though a couple of prime suspects like you and Bruno corroborating each other's alibis wouldn't impress a jury, the fact that people at the hotel saw you coming and going—assuming they did—would probably be enough to establish your whereabouts somewhere other than at the scene of the abduction and murder. And, I guess, Scooter would testify as to your whereabouts."

He got trembly again. "Oh, Jesus, poor Scooter. I shouldn't have let him come. I never liked threesomes, but I knew Bruno wouldn't mind, so I let him talk me into it. If the station finds out about Scooter, they'll have him sweeping the newsroom floor for the rest of the term of his contract. But he wanted to come. He has this thing about watching weathermen being—you know. Scooter's a little weird."

"Bruno mentioned that. What is it about Bruno you find so attractive, Ronnie?"

A puzzled look. "You don't think he's attractive?"

"That kind of thing is pretty subjective."

"Well, for me it's his charisma."

"That's not a word I'd have come up with for Bruno."

"You know," he said, gesturing vaguely, "his power and glamour. Somebody who's in his natural element

155

when he's in the media eye. Bruno is brilliant and aggressive—and God is he butch. I get goosebumps just thinking about him."

"Have you ever been involved with that type of man before?"

His body tightened. "Sure. I've gotten lucky a couple of times."

I looked at him and said, "Who was the last powerful, butch man in your life?"

Sweat popped out on his forehead and he looked away. "I can't tell you that."

"You can't, or you won't?"

"I can't. And I won't, ever. That subject doesn't have anything to do with John Rutka, so drop it. What else do you want to know?"

"I'm getting the idea there was a connection between your last boyfriend and John Rutka. Maybe his name is in Rutka's file on you. I'll have to go back and check."

He shook his head. "No. He was too careful. There's no way John Rutka could have known about this man. It won't be in my file, I'm sure. You'd be wasting your time with this man. Take my word for it." Sweat was dribbling off his nose.

"In your file," I said, "there's a note that says you were at a certain motel with someone referred to as 'A' once a week for nearly a year up until mid-June. Was that your boyfriend?"

Tears slid down his face. "I can't take this."

"Was 'A' one of his initials?"

He shook his head and wept silently.

I said, "If John Rutka had known about this man and had been preparing to out him, what would the consequences have been?"

He pulled a perfect white handkerchief out of his back pocket and mopped the tears and sweat from his face.

"Awful," he said. "It would have been— Oh, God. Look, I can't talk about this anymore. I really can't."

"Just tell me this, Ronnie. What would this man's reaction have been if he had been outed?"

He sat there for a long moment shaking his head again, when suddenly he gave a furious shudder, yanked up the sleeve of his jacket, and thrust his left wrist in front of my face.

"Do you see that?" he rasped.

I stared at the scar.

"Ten years ago I had enough of a world full of people like you. If you keep pushing me, Strachey, I'll do it again. And I'll leave a note blaming you."

"No need for that," I said.

"I mean it!"

"I can see you do. I believe you."

"And this time nobody will find me."

"Hey, I'm cool."

"Are you going to stop leaning on me?"

"Yup."

"Is that a promise?"

"I promise."

"How can I believe you?" he said desperately, and flung himself back against his seat.

"I'll take you back to Channel Eight now, Ronnie, if that's where you want to go, and I won't bother you anymore. You'll see."

He sat there for another minute catching his breath, while I spoke to him reassuringly. Finally he interrupted me and said, "Oh, let's have some breakfast." And he got instantly out of the car.

Inside, Linkletter grinned as people throughout the crowded restaurant recognized him and said Hello, and Have a nice day, and I just washed my car so I guess it's gonna rain, huh? Ronnie thought that last one was a knee-slapper.

After breakfast, as I drove back to Channel Eight, we chatted about baseball and of course the weather. Linkletter said the next twenty-four hours would be nice, and I was about to say, "Hey, that's the way we like it," and then thought better of it and just said thanks.

So much for Ronnie Linkletter as a route to the Mega-Hypocrite.

20

The Fountain of Eden Motel on Route 5 was an old clapboard house with a neon sign on the roof and a long "L" of fifteen single-story shingled motel units appended to its backside. The office was in the back of the house, and you could pull around and ease up to it without being seen from the highway.

A wooden door with a patched screen led into a registration alcove. The tiny room, which stank of the nicotine stains that gummed the walls, contained a wooden counter, a condom machine, and no chairs. I pressed a button on the counter and could hear a buzzer sound in the inner reaches of the house.

"She's out back!" The male voice was muffled but the words decipherable.

"Whereabouts?" I yelled back.

"Doin' the laundry. Past number six."

I found an open door to a small room squeezed in between units six and seven. A squat, middle-aged woman in shorts and a T-shirt was stuffing sheets into a washing machine, a filtered cigarette dangling from the corner of her mouth. She was blond and sad-eyed and had a long-lost pretty face somewhere. The cigarette was lighted and her breathing sounded like somebody walking around in a swamp.

"You want a room?"

"How much until noon?"

"Eighteen."

I gave her a twenty and got back two that came from the shorts pocket. The twenty went in there with her wad. She took a key out of her other pocket and said, "I just made up eleven."

"Should I register?"

"No need to."

"What if I stole something—walked off with your television? The rooms have TV, don't they?"

"Sure. VCRs too. But if anybody steals anything, we can get it back. Are you planning on stealing something? You better not."

"How come?"

"I know your license number." She recited it. "I looked at it while you were inside the office and I'll write it down when I get back to the desk. If we need to get ahold of you for anything, we can find you through the DMV. People who stay here usually'd rather not leave their names, but we can track you down if we want you. Jay handles it."

"I don't plan on stealing anything," I said, "but I'd like to speak with Jay when he comes in. Would you give him this?"

"Sure."

I handed her the sealed envelope containing the note I wrote to Gladu after I drove Ronnie Linkletter back to Channel Eight. I went out and pulled the car over to number 11. Only two other cars were in the lot, a new Acura and an old Ford Galaxie in front of units 3 and 4. I checked the mud flaps on both; all four were intact.

160

Room 11 was small and dim with thick curtains drawn shut. A water bed in a lacquered pine frame that matched the paneling on one wall took up much of the room. The print on the filthy bedspread showed pastoral vistas and Georgian mansions. The TV set on the dresser was hooked up to the discount store–brand VCR beside it. Two walls of the room were covered with mirrors, as was the ceiling above the bed. The towels beside the small sink outside the bathroom were worn but clean. Above the sink an ancient contraption of an air conditioner was jammed into what had been a window. When I switched it to "on," nothing happened.

I'd brought the *Times* along and sat by a low-watt lamp in the airless room plugging away at the crossword puzzle—one of those with puns so dumb you wanted to call up Sulzberger and ask for your fifty cents back—until just after ten, when a knock came at the door.

I opened it and a thirtyish groover in baggy black shirt and pants and jackboots grinned at me a little too brilliantly out of a pale smooth face. "Are you the blackmailer?"

"Yup."

"How much do you want? If it's too much, I may have to have you killed."

He was still grinning, contented with his existence and mine, and apparently not prepared to take me as much of a threat. He seemed to be a man who had found inner peace, though whether its provenance was spiritual or chemical I didn't know.

"I don't want your money," I said. "I just want to find out who killed John Rutka, and I thought you might be able to help me out, Jay."

"I don't think so."

I sat in my chair again and Gladu flopped onto the water bed and arranged the pillows behind his back.

161

"John Rutka paid you more than six thousand dollars last year," I said. "What for?"

"No, he didn't."

"It's in his financial records—the amounts of the disbursements and the dates."

"That might be in John Rutka's financial records, but it's not in mine. There are no canceled checks. You won't find my signature anywhere in John Rutka's records. Or in anyone else's. Except New York Telephone's, of course. I'm a phone-company subscriber and proud of it. The power company too."

"I see your point. On the other hand," I said, "there's an exceptionally large number of references to the Fountain of Eden in the files Rutka kept on gay Albanians he was planning to out. In all of the files, the Fountain of Eden comes up eighty or ninety times. Apparently someone here was feeding Rutka information on the assorted couplings and quadruplings that the participants, your paying customers, assumed to be private. If the police or the tax authorities had possession of those files—which they do not, yet—they might imagine a connection existed between the cash disbursements and the carefully indexed sexual reports. They'd think poorly of you, as would your customers once word got around. Your business inevitably would suffer."

He shrugged and peered at me brightly. "This place is not my only source of income. I've got an art gallery in Woodstock and a pet shop in the Millpond Mall. But don't get me wrong. I get your point. What is it you'd like to know?"

"I'd like to know who came to the Fountain of Eden with Ronnie Linkletter every Wednesday night for a year. I'd like you to instruct whoever it is on your staff here who keeps track of these things to talk to me and to answer truthfully every question I ask. And I want to

162

leave here with copies of your license-plate records for the past year. Arrange those few things and we'll call it even."

"What do you mean, 'even'? What's in it for me?"

"After whoever killed John Rutka is caught, Rutka's records will be destroyed. I'll do it myself. All those embarrassing connections to you and your business will be gone."

A dry laugh. "Do I look embarrassed?"

"Not yet."

"Well, maybe instead of doing all those things you're demanding I do, I should do what I first thought when Sandy gave me your threatening note. I should just arrange to have you killed." He grinned.

"Is that something you do to people routinely, or would I be receiving exceptional treatment?"

"I can't answer that. It would be giving something away."

Hoping I was guessing right about Gladu, I said, "I'm not impressed with your chemically induced bravado, Jay, and I'm getting bored with your line of utter bullshit. I want answers and I want them now. Who do I talk to around here to get them?"

He blinked twice, tapped his fingers on the bed frame, and said, "You can talk to me. I have the answers to your questions, and I'll give you the answers in return for one thousand dollars."

I sighed. "Jay, how would you like *Cityscape* to do a story on the Fountain of Eden as the Albany area's most popular quickie heaven, where the elite meet to fornicate, except the management spies on the customers and sells the information to political dementos like John Rutka and also tries to sell it to private investigators working on murder cases? The story would be a natural for *Cityscape,* and I'd be happy to supply the paper with the evidence that would pretty much put you out of business."

"I'd hate that," he said with a little slit of a smile and the same bright eyes. "If that happened, somebody might arrange to kill *me.*"

"Could be."

"I have to admit, Strachey, that you've got me backed into a corner. So I've decided that I will answer your questions." His eyes got even brighter. "And then *later* I'll arrange to have you killed. Months from now, or even years, when you're least suspecting it. You'll be walking down Lark Street. Or you'll be home doing some blow, or you'll have your tongue wrapped around your boy-friend's willy, or you'll be lying in bed looking through *Mirabella.* And all of a sudden—ka-*powie!*—you're a piece of Center Square roadkill!"

I said, "You're full of shit, Gladu."

"You think I am, don't you?"

"Yes."

"You're right." He guffawed.

"I know."

"What were the questions you wanted answered? I forgot."

"First, tell me how it worked—your data-gathering methods. Who were the actual spies?"

"Sandy in the daytime picks up quite a bit. She's got the tube on all the time and remembers faces, so when some local mega-celeb shows up she'll spot him right away and make a note of it. She gets five bucks a pop for a regular spotting, ten for media heavies like Ronnie Linkletter. I've got two queens who alternate nights—Royce and Lemuel, who live over in the house—and they know everbody and don't miss a trick. They're devastated that Rutka is dead, because now there's nobody to sell their dirt to."

164

"They knew the dirt was going to Rutka?"

"Sure, I told them. Not that they cared. A dollar is a dollar. Being a bitch is being a bitch whether it's politically correct or not. For them, it's just a hoot."

I said, "I've been through Rutka's files, Jay. And I have a pretty good fix on who was spotted here, and when, and who they were with, and what kind of lubricants were left behind, and used condoms in the linen and on the floor, and roaches in the ashtrays, and all the rest of the detritus of hundreds of happy romps at the Fountain of Eden. What I'd like is any additional information you can give me on one man in particular: Ronnie Linkletter."

Gladu sniffed a couple of times to clear his nostrils and his mind. "I knew you were going to ask about Ronnie."

"Why?"

"Because I thought maybe he had something to do with Rutka getting offed."

"You thought Ronnie did it?"

"No—not that he was actually the one."

"Then what? What made you think of Ronnie at all?"

Gladu sat forward now and struggled to stay in focus. "Well, for one thing, Ronnie was one of the people John was really after—somebody he just had to uncloset. There were these three people John used to talk about as the dudes he wanted to get the most. One was Bruno Slinger, on account of how he helped kill the queer-bashing law or whatever that was. When John finally got Slinger he was high for a month. Of the three big assholes on his list, Bruno was the first one outed. Then Ronnie was the one he wanted, partly because he was so popular in Albany, and famous, but there was another reason, too."

"What was that?"

"It had something to do with Ronnie's boyfriend, somebody he met here every Wednesday night from

165

seven till ten, when he had to get back to Channel Eight and get the weather report ready for the eleven o'clock news. When John found out who the boyfriend was, then he *really* wanted to get Ronnie."

"Who was the boyfriend?"

"I don't know. I thought I knew, but I guess I don't actually know."

"Explain that, please."

He was sitting cross-legged in the center of the bed now, rocking gently, and measuring his words. "Well," he said, "the boyfriend always arrived after dark in a raincoat with the collar turned up and wearing a baseball cap with the brim pulled down."

"What team?"

"Nobody ever got close enough to see anything like that. Although Lemuel and Royce tried their best to get a look. But they were never quick enough. The dude would drive in after Ronnie was already here and the room was paid for, and he'd slip inside the room with the curtains shut. They were always in unit fifteen, down at the end. Ronnie would reserve it and Lemuel or Royce would hold it even if we got busy, because Ronnie and his honey were always punctual."

"How did Rutka find out who Ronnie's boyfriend was if Lemuel and Royce didn't even know?"

"Through the license plate of the car he drove. We had that much. John and I both have DMV contacts and we found out who owned the car. It's some nobody in Pine Hills. I've got his name written down over in the office. I don't know how, but John figured out that Ronnie's mystery boyfriend was somebody who borrowed this other guy's car every Wednesday night, and it was somebody he wanted to drag out of the closet even more than Bruno and Ronnie. He got Bruno, and then he got Ronnie. But I don't think he ever outed the third one, the one

166

he wanted the most. I'm not sure why, but I think John was scared of this one."

"What makes you think so?"

"From the way he talked. He always referred to this one as the All-American Mega-Hypocrite. He was some hot-shit something-or-other who was a deep closet case, and I got the impression he was one dangerous asshole."

"Did he threaten John?"

"No, I don't think he even knew John was onto him. John never said so, anyway. For a while John was always working on a way to get a picture of Ronnie and the Mega-Hypocrite in bed, or a tape or something. But I wouldn't go along with that. I didn't want anything traceable to me or my business. You don't stay in the motel business pulling shit like that."

Mr. Situational Ethics. I said, "When did Ronnie and the mystery man break up? Or did they? It's Ronnie's story that they broke up."

"All I know is," Gladu said, "they stopped coming here about two months ago, and it wasn't long after that that I heard Ronnie and Bruno, John's first- and second-favorite outees, were getting it on together at the Parmalee Plaza. Well, that's cozy, I remember thinking. I don't know what became of Mr. Mega-Hypocrite. Maybe he scared Ronnie off too. Though with Ronnie, it looks like the bigger and meaner they are, the stiffer his dick."

"It looks that way."

"At the time, I thought maybe they didn't come back here because of what happened in unit fifteen later that night after they were here for the last time. But I don't see how they could have known about it. We kept it quiet. You didn't hear anything, did you? It's not in John's files, is it?" He looked apprehensive.

"I don't know if it's in the files, because I don't know what you're referring to, Jay. Clue me in."

A pause. Then: "The mirror fell off the ceiling in unit fifteen. I guess all those hours of fucking over the years loosened some screws and one whole six-by-four-foot section of mirror over the bed in that unit dropped off. If anybody had been in the bed at the time, they could have been killed."

We both looked up at the mirror above Gladu and winced. Long metal flanges held the mirror sections in place. It looked as if the flanges were screwed into the old ceiling beams. We saw ourselves up there looking back at ourselves with nauseated looks.

I said, "How does your insurance company feel about those mirrors?"

He looked queasy. "They don't know about them, actually."

"Ah."

"The mirrors have all been tightened up. Hey, if you ever bring a trick out here, you won't have to worry."

"I happen to be in a monogamous situation, but thanks for the reassurance."

"Maybe you and your boyfriend would like to come out for a weekend getaway sometime. We have special weekend rates."

"What are they, higher?"

"Naturally."

I said, "Who was working here the night the mirror fell?"

"Royce. Poor Royce was wrecked for a week."

"I'd like to speak to him. Is he here?"

"Over in the house."

"Is Royce his first name or his last?"

"It's Royce McClosky."

"Do you know who D.R. is?"

"D.R.?"

"The initials D.R."

He thought about this. "Donna Reed?"

168

"I don't think so. Who besides you was John Rutka paying to spy on people and feed dirt to him for his outing files?"

"That's confidential, but since you're blackmailing me, I'll tell you. Nathan Zenck at the Parmalee Plaza was paid, I know."

"Just Zenck?"

"He's the only one I know of. I know Nathan. He's a silly queen but an excellent businessman. We're different but we have a lot of respect for each other."

I told him I wanted to look at his license-plate records and we walked over to the office. I bent down briefly to check the mud flaps on Gladu's Mercedes. Both were intact. Inside the registration alcove, Gladu flipped up the hinged end of the counter and went behind it to rummage through some drawers. He produced a long box of index cards with dates, times, and license-plate numbers written on them.

"Some people we actually register. The state says we have to," Gladu said, and brought out a much smaller box of registration cards filled in with probably mostly phony names and addresses. "We like to respect people's privacy," he said, "so not everyone is required to register, and all transactions are in cash."

"What crap. You cheat the state and federal governments out of the taxes and you sell information on people's private lives for additional cash."

He suddenly glared at me and slammed his left fist on the counter. His other hand came up from behind the counter with a .38 caliber revolver, which he aimed at me. "Now I am going to see that you die, you scumbag blackmailer, and I'm going to do it myself right now!"

"Gladu, just shut up and get me the files. And put that thing away before it goes off and the rest of your mirrors drop."

He chuckled and put the gun back under the counter.

"Where's Royce?" I said.

Gladu pressed the buzzer on the counter.

"She's out back!" came a voice from above.

"Royce is off-duty now. He's probably watching Geraldo with Lemuel and wishes not to be disturbed. But I guess you're going to insist on disturbing him."

"Yes, I am."

"Royce, get down here!" Gladu yelled. "A blackmailer wants to talk to you."

He placed the two file boxes on the counter along with a sheet of paper on which was written a license-plate number, a name, and an address.

"Who's this? The owner of the car Ronnie Linkletter's mystery man came in?"

"That's what John told me. But not the man himself, according to John."

The name on the paper was Art Murphy, and the address was 37 Flint Street, Albany, a short street I'd passed a thousand times that ran off Washington Avenue in the old Pine Hills section of the city. Art Murphy did not sound like an arch-hypocrite, but maybe Art regularly lent or rented his car to a man who was. I wondered if Art had ever been blackmailed and if he ever thought he would be.

"This man's name is Strachey," Gladu told Royce when he appeared. "He's a pond-scum degenerate black-mailer, and as your employer I am directing you to answer every question he asks you. Later I'm going to have him killed, but for now tell him whatever he wants to know." Gladu beamed.

Royce, a skinny, bleary-eyed man in his fifties with a stubble of beard, and mouthwash on his breath, looked at me uncertainly and then back at Gladu. "Tell him what, Jay?"

"Anything. Everything. I told you—he'll never live to use any of it against any of us."

170

"Let's go outside," I told Royce.

Royce didn't like the sound of that. He looked as if he had last been exposed to sunlight in the year of the Watergate break-in, but Gladu beamed contentedly and motioned for Royce to move out.

I carried the Fountain of Eden registration and license-plate files with me, and we sat in my car with both doors open.

"Where you going with those?" Royce asked.

"I'll bring them back eventually," I said, "so not to worry. The only thing you need to concern yourself with, Royce, is doing what Jay said and telling me the absolute truth on all the topics I bring up. Okay?"

"Sure."

"Who got hit with the mirror?"

He'd been looking bewildered up to now, and only vaguely apprehensive, but now his eyes narrowed and he looked at me with suspicion tinged with dread.

"Who are you?" he said. "Are you a cop?"

"No, I'm just a blackmailer. I have tons and tons of incriminating crap on Jay, so you better answer my questions or he'll be ruined and you will too. This is all off the books, and I know you're used to that, Royce, so let's get on with it and everything will be cool. Once again, who got hit with the mirror?"

"How did you know about that? If you were one of the people who came out that night, you'd know who it was. If you're not one of them, how did you know it happened? Jay doesn't know, or even Sandy. Lemmie didn't tell you, did he?"

I said, "Nobody had to tell me. Linkletter and his boyfriend were here every Wednesday night for almost a year, and then the mirror fell and they stopped coming. Jay swallowed your story that the mirror fell after Ronnie and his friend had left because Jay has a lot invested emotionally and financially in believing that that's the way it happened. But it's mighty unlikely that Ronnie's failure to come back to his habitual trysting place ever again is mere coincidence. How much did they pay you to keep your mouth shut?"

"Two hundred dollars," he said, brushing away a sweat bead from the end of his nose with a trembling hand.

"Who was hit? The boyfriend?"

He gulped and nodded.

"Who was he?"

He shook his head. "I never saw him—that night or ever. I don't know who the heck he was."

"Did he die? Was he killed by the falling mirror?"

"I don't know. Ronnie called somebody from the pay phone and they came and carried the guy out and took him away in a car. They gave Ronnie the money to give to me for keeping my mouth shut, and since I didn't know anything about the man, it was no problem keeping mum. And Ronnie said it was okay, just tell Jay the mirror fell afterwards, so that's what I did."

"Ronnie wasn't hurt?"

"Just shook up. He had some scratches but he was— well, he was underneath at the time the mirror fell. The other guy was the one who really got clobbered."

"The mystery man was fucking Ronnie when it happened?"

"That's what Ronnie said."

"How long did it take after Ronnie phoned for help for somebody to show up?"

"Ten, fifteen minutes maybe."

"Were there other customers here at the time? Were there other witnesses to what happened next?"

"There were people here but I don't think anybody even took notice. People don't come here to mind other people's business. They come here to take care of their own business and they're usually busy with whatever that business is—very personal."

"Who arrived? How many? In what vehicle or vehicles?"

"I watched out the window from the office," Royce said, glancing around to see if anyone was looking our way. "Ronnie said I should stay away and what I didn't know wouldn't hurt me. There was just one car, with three men in it. I didn't get a very good look at them—they stayed down by unit fifteen where it happened—but it was a cool night and I could see they had on long coats with their collars turned up. Nice dress coats like businessmen would wear, or gangsters. All of a sudden it hit me while I'm standing there looking out the window that these guys might be from the mob! And the guy who's fucking Ronnie every Wednesday night is some friggin' godfather or something. For a minute I just sat down and didn't even look. But then I got curious again and I looked."

"What did you see next?"

"Well, they sent Ronnie over with the two hundred and said this was for keeping my mouth shut, and I said sure, okay. They never came to the office themselves. They just loaded the boyfriend into the back seat of this big white Chrysler they came in, and one of them drove the car the boyfriend brought—his usual shiny blue Olds—and then they left. Ronnie left in his car, and I went in and wiped up the blood—there wasn't a whole lot—and then I locked up the unit until I told Jay the next day that the mirror in fifteen fell after Ronnie left." He gave me a pleading look. "You aren't going to tell Jay I lied, are you?"

"I don't see why. You've been honest with me, so I guess I can do you a favor and be dishonest with Jay."

173

"Thanks. He's a real schmuck. Are you really black-mailing him?"

"Yup."

"Well, good luck. He deserves it."

"I'm doing my best."

"Swell."

I said, "Did you get the license-plate number of the Chrysler? Everybody out here seems to be pretty thorough about that."

"Nope. I didn't. I tried."

"Why couldn't you?"

"Because the plates were taped over, front and back. Whoever these people were, they sure went to a lot of trouble to make sure they weren't identified. Do you have any idea who they were?"

I said no, and for once that day I was telling somebody the truth. I didn't know who the men in the nice dress coats had been, but I thought Art Murphy probably would.

21

Flint Street ran for two blocks off Washington and dead-ended at a medical-records warehouse. The street was shady and quiet, and the frame houses were set close together in a way that probably felt neighborly to some of the people who lived there and claustrophobic to some of the others.

Number 37, like all the houses on the block, was a two-story job with a deep, boxy front porch and a small patch of sparse lawn that didn't get much sunlight or rain. No car was parked in the narrow driveway and none of those on the street fit the description—a shiny blue Olds—or bore the license-plate number of the car the Mega-Hypocrite had driven out to the Fountain of Eden every Wednesday night until the mirror fell on him.

The main front door was open at number 37, with only a screen door to keep out the insects and the blackmailers. I got the feeling Art Murphy wasn't home, and this was confirmed when I drove over to a convenience store with a pay phone, on Washington. Murphy was listed in the Albany directory, and I dialed the number on Flint Street.

A female voice, not young, a tad nasal. "Hello?"

"Art Murphy, please?"

"Oh, Arthur isn't at home at this hour. He'd be at work."

"This is Jim Smith and I'm in town and Art asked me to get in touch. May I have his work number, please?"

"Yes, that would be Byrne Olds-Cadillac," she said, and recited the number.

"Thank you—Mrs. Murphy?"

"Why, yes."

"Have a nice day."

I dialed the number. "Good morning. Byrne Olds-Cadillac."

"Is Art Murphy over there today? Don't ring him—I want to drop by."

"Art's in the showroom. He'll be around, I'm pretty sure."

"Thanks."

I drove back over to Central and west toward Colonie. Byrne Olds-Cadillac was one of the patriotic GM dealers that hadn't taken on a Japanese line to keep the customers coming, but had clung to a tattered domestic respectability untouched by Asia's peculiar ways and well-made economical vehicles. A gigantic American flag hung from a pole next to the entrance, and the place looked proud but not busy.

No one rushed out to pound my Mitsubishi with a sledgehammer as I pulled in; I parked on the far side of the lot where the other parked cars had no sales stickers and appeared to belong to employees. I found the shiny blue Olds in no time at all, checked the license plate, which matched the one Jay Gladu had given me for the mysterious Wednesday-night motel visitor's car, and then checked the mud flaps, front and rear. All were intact and none seemed newly replaced. I crawled

176

around a second time and examined them. The two front flaps were identical, and appropriately worn, as were the two rear flaps. So this was probably not the murder car. But its owner, I was confident, would know whose was.

I went into the showroom and approached a middle-aged man in a mint-green blazer with slicked-back gray hair.

"Art Murphy?"

"Yessir."

"I'm Don Strachey and I'd like to talk to you about a car. Somebody told me that you're the man to see."

"I'd like to think I know a little bit about cars. What would you be interested in, Mr.—Straker?"

"Strachey."

"Sorry about that."

"There's one particular car I'd like to discuss with you. The blue Olds out in the lot that belongs to you and that was driven out to the Fountain of Eden Motel every Wednesday night for nearly a year. Could we go somewhere private and talk about that car?"

We were standing alongside a Cadillac that didn't at all resemble the boatlike ostentatious vessels the name has always evoked and will always evoke for North Americans born before a certain year. But this Cadillac was big enough to hold Art Murphy up when he fell back as if he'd been struck and then leaned against it trying to catch his breath.

"What the fuck you wanna do to me?"

"Do you have an office, Art? You look as if you need to sit down."

He hesitated, staring at me, then reddened and gestured for me to follow. We went into his glassed-in cubicle and he shut the door. He sat behind his desk and loosened his tie, still breathing with effort, and kept glancing around to see who might be watching. A man

177

who looked like a younger Art was in a cubicle two doors down, busy with some papers, and he didn't seem to be aware of the distress bordering on panic that his colleague was suffering.

"Who the fuck are you?"

"Don Strachey, a private investigator. I'm trying to find out, among other things, who killed John Rutka."

"Killed who? Who'd you say?" He was sweating and kept squirming and loosening things, but none of it seemed to help.

"Who used your car every Wednesday night? Or was that you out there boffing the Channel Eight weatherman in unit fifteen every week until the night the mirror fell? If it was you, Art, you sure look none the worse for wear. Except it wasn't you, was it? You don't quite qualify as a mega-hypocrite."

"Who *told* you this horseshit?"

"And now whoever it is you're protecting, Art, has killed John Rutka, the man who had the goods on him and was planning on exposing his nauseating hypocrisy. Art, do you know what the penalty is in the State of New York for obstructing the investigation of a homicide?"

The sweat still flowed, but now he was getting a confused look. "Mister, I don't know what the hell you are talking about. Is John Rutka that gay kid on the news who was murdered?"

"I think we both know well enough who John Rutka was."

"You're nuts, that's what you are! I wouldn't know John Rutka from Adam. You are just plain nuts."

I sat there gazing at Murphy in his state of agitated confusion, and now I was starting to get a little confused myself. "Do you deny that your car was parked outside unit fifteen at the Fountain of Eden Motel every Wednesday night for most of the past year from seven P.M. to ten P.M.?"

178

He reddened again and said nothing for a long moment. Then: "What I do with my car and who drives it is none of your goddamn business. And what I do with my car has nothing to do with any goddamn murder, and I'd like to know how you think there's any connection. I dare you—I dare you to tell me how there is any connection between my car and who drives it and any damn murder!"

This was not going the way I had thought it would. "Art, I've got all the evidence I need to connect your car with the motel, and with the man who went there every Wednesday night to meet Ronnie Linkletter and to know him carnally. And while I am happy to acknowledge that such same-sex carnal knowledge is no longer a criminal act in the State of New York—unlike twenty-five other barbaric states—and while I share your opinion that what went on at the Fountain of Eden is none of my damned business—or yours—still, there is this: Certain evidence connects the man who used your car to the abduction and murder of John Rutka last Wednesday night. You can tell me now what you know, or you can talk to the Handbag police an hour from now after I phone them. Take your pick."

"Now I *know* you're nuts. There couldn't be any connection between my car and a murder—when?"

"Wednesday, two nights ago."

"Im-*possible.* I don't know where you're getting your information, but you have been *mis-in-formed.* Nope, you're all wet, that's what you are, mister."

He glanced defiantly at his watch, then sat there eyeing me, his breathing evener now, but still wary and scared. Murphy hadn't denied that his car had been at the Fountain of Eden Motel every Wednesday night, or that its user had been hit by a falling mirror; he only denied that the man had—or even could have had—any connection with the kidnaping and murder of John Rutka.

179

It hit me with a cold thud deep inside that I might have been on the wrong trail all along, that Ronnie Linkletter's boyfriend who got clobbered with the mirror might not have been the Mega-Hypocrite whose file was missing (even though Ronnie himself had acted as if the man had been), or if he had—or even hadn't—the Mega-Hypocrite wasn't the murderer at all, and the missing file was part of an elaborate ploy meant to throw investigators off the track. But if so, whose ploy?

I had one last go at Art Murphy. I said, "Art, I can only present my evidence to the police, of course, but I think I've told you enough to convince you that you're in this not up to your neck but certainly up to your knees. Just tell me: Who borrowed your car every Wednesday night until mid-June, when the mirror fell? Tell me that, Art, and we might be able to keep the police out of this. I'm not promising anything, but I'll do my best to see that your employer and family don't have to hear about your involvement in this sordid affair."

He grimaced at that last cheap shot, but he also sensed my diminished confidence and the incompleteness of my chain of evidence. "I told you, who uses my car is none of your goddamn business, and I'll also tell you this: Anybody who might've borrowed my car anytime certainly did not have anything to do with a murder last Wednesday night, that's for goddamn sure."

"Is he dead? Was he killed by the falling mirror?"

He got red again. "I told you, buster, none of that is any of your business, and I'm not about to say a word about it. It's not connected to this Rutka guy, so I don't have to tell you or the police a goddamn thing, and I'm not about to, either."

"You'd refuse to cooperate with the police, Art? An upstanding citizen like yourself? What would your boss think? Old Bill Byrne? Wouldn't old Bill be disappointed in you?"

He'd had enough of me. "Get out of here! I want you out of here *now!"*

"If I refuse to leave, will you call the police?"

"I'll call the goddamn Albany police. I have friends in the department and I can tell you right now, if they come out here they'll make hamburger out of you, all right. You better just beat it, buster. Go on!"

"Hey, no need to get nasty about it." I got up.

He stood, trembling, and pointed at me. "You said you were a private investigator. Is that the truth?"

"Yes, it is."

"Well, who you working for, anyway? Who hired you?"

"That's confidential."

He glared at me, red-faced again. Then suddenly he started shaking his head and his arms and waving everything away—me, the papers on his desk, whoever had gotten him into this. He just shook and waved, shook and waved. He was mad as hell and he wasn't going to take it anymore, except all he knew to do was stand there and shake and wave, shake and wave.

I left him like that and went out and drove away. I hoped Art Murphy didn't have a stroke or a heart attack, and I wished my headache, which was back, would go away and stay away too.

22

I was mixed up and it was time to stop and think. Whether or not Ronnie Linkletter's boyfriend was the All-American Asshole Mega-Hypocrite—and Ronnie's behavior suggested strongly that he was—and whether or not the Mega-Hypocrite had committed the murder of John Rutka—and he was still the most logical suspect despite the missing files maybe being a part of a scheme to frame whoever the mirror man turned out to be—I knew I couldn't begin to confirm or eliminate Linkletter's falling-mirror man as anything at all—Mega-Hypocrite, murderer, victim of a frame-up—until I knew his identity and could check his mud flaps and his alibi or lack of one for Wednesday night.

Assuming for the time being that the motel mystery man was the Mega-Hypocrite, I needed to know if he was even alive.

I drove into town and went into the Albany Public Library. I checked all the obituaries in the *Times Union* file for mid-June. No pillars of the community had expired on or soon after the date of the falling mirror. Any number of those who had joined the majority during this period—Mrs. Tillie Levitsky, age eighty-seven; Franklin Moneypenny, age ninety-four; Arline M. Reilly, age one hundred and three; and several dozen others—might well have been considered hypocrites by their survivors if it came out that they had been spending Wednesday nights in a Central Avenue hot-sheet motel. But not mega-hypocrites whose hypocrisy was so monstrous as to earn them a place at the top of Rutka's list of danger-to-society closet cases.

Then a headline about a gangland shooting on the front page of a mid-June *T-U* caught my eye, and for a few excited minutes I thought I'd figured it all out. From a pay phone, I called an acquaintance in New York City who specializes in the intricacies of mob life. I asked him if any Mafia figure might have visited Albany every Wednesday night for a year until mid-June, and if such a figure might have then died or disappeared with no explanation.

The reporter said no, none of that made any sense. No major mob figure needed to visit Albany (which didn't even have a good clam house), since those politicians beholden to the mob traveled without objection to wherever their bosses were situated, making it unnecessary for their bosses to journey out to visit them. Nor had any major mid-level mobster in the Northeast died or disappeared during the month of June, other than the one I'd just read about who'd been gunned down while visiting Miami. I thanked the reporter for his disappointing information and hung up.

The mirror man, I decided, was probably alive. Though maybe badly scarred. Maybe what I had to find was a deeply closeted gay man with hideous scars on his back and buttocks. Maybe the state police could put out an all-points bulletin. Or I could go around pulling down the pants of respectably dressed gay men and checking their buttocks. I felt as though that's what I was about to be reduced to.

Back at the house on Crow Street, I slapped together a two-day-old-runny-tuna sandwich and ate it with two aspirin. Two messages were on my machine, one from Joel McClurg at *Cityscape* reminding me of our agreement that I'd tip him off if I was closing in on the killer—I thought, Fat chance of my doing that any time soon—and one message from Bub Bailey asking me to phone him with any new leads I'd come up with and telling me that he, regrettably, had none. He said he hoped to see me at the Rutka funeral the next morning and we'd catch up on each other's developments.

While I was eating, Federal Express showed up with a package from New York City. I signed for it and set it on the kitchen counter, unopened.

After lunch, I got out my list of local sources and worked the phone. Art Murphy still seemed like the best route to the identity of the motel-mirror man, so I got busy trying to find out who Art hung around with, who his family members were, and who he might lend his car to every night for a year.

Art's credit was in order, I learned, and he owned his house on Flint Street, with just two years to go on the mortgage. Art was sixty-one years old. The credit agency was also able to tell me that Art earned $42,570 the previous year, that his outstanding debts were a Key Bank car loan with monthly payments of $289, and that his unpaid Visa balance was $721. A second card-holder was a Mrs. June Murphy, age fifty-nine, same address as Art.

Through a friend in the school department records office, I found out that the Murphys had three daughters, Linda, Connie, and Joyce, who, I calculated, would now

184

be thirty-eight, thirty-seven, and thirty-one. None was listed in the Albany phone book; they'd either married and changed their names, or moved away, or all had unlisted numbers. Or maybe they all lived at home with Art and June, happy never to leave the simple pleasures of Flint Street.

I used the street address—name of occupant guide to search for an acquaintance of mine in Art's neighborhood, but could find none. I was luckier, though, when I phoned a friend who was a bookkeeper for another car dealer up the highway from Byrne Olds-Cadillac; he told me he knew Art only slightly, but his brother had a friend who had once dated one of Art's daughters and he'd have the brother's friend give me a call, if he could reach him, which he did. The friend, Lou Ptak, soon called, a tad suspicious of who or what I was, which he should have been.

I told him I worked for the Federal Bureau of Investigation and one of Art's daughters had applied for a position with the agency, necessitating a full-field security check.

"Which daughter?" Lou Ptak asked.

"Joyce," I said, taking a chance, and he started laughing. "It figures," he said, and chortled off and on throughout our conversation.

The Murphys' family life was unexceptional, according to Ptak. Art and June had devoted their lives to raising their daughters, all of whom had fled Albany at the earliest opportunity. Ptak didn't know who Art's friends were, but he thought they were the men from Byrne Olds-Cadillac and those who shared Art's interests in golf and bowling.

Art's parents were dead, Ptak thought, and June's mother was perhaps living, but in a nursing home. The extended Murphy family, he didn't know. When I asked if any of them might have achieved local renown, he said that was a funny question for the FBI to be asking, but he thought not. Ptak said he hadn't actually been in touch with the family for ten years, since Joyce broke up with him and announced that she had decided to become a nun. Then he laughed again, and was still chuckling when we both hung up.

I called Timmy at his office and said, "I'm flummoxed. I've spent the day threatening and badgering and attempting to blackmail people who probably don't deserve it. John Rutka would have been proud of me, going around terrorizing all kinds of poor bastards who mainly just want to be left alone to work a few of the harmless scams the republic is founded on and then at the end of the day climb into bed with some simpatico struggling soul and get a little comfort. I did all that and got nowhere and ended up with next to nothing." I described my meetings with Ronnie Linkletter, Jay Gladu, Royce McClosky, and the hapless car-lender Art Murphy.

"That doesn't sound like a washout to me," Timmy said. "Slinger told you last night that Linkletter's old boyfriend was top-secret stuff, and Ronnie confirmed it, and Ronnie also confirmed that the guy is someone very, very formidable—so formidable that Ronnie would not be able to stand the big man's exposure. If that isn't a perfect profile of Rutka's Mega-Hypocrite, I don't know who would be better. I think you're close."

"Maybe I am. It's just that I'm sick of it all."

"And the stuff that the motel people told you—the way the mirror man was spirited away in a big white Chrysler with taped plates. That sure sounds like a mega-hypocrite."

"Yeah."

"Did you just call me up to whine?"

"I guess I did."

186

"Maybe you need to take a break, get some distance on the whole thing."

"Nah, that never works for me. The picture doesn't clarify, it just blurs. I'll have to keep at it."

"You've got my sympathy and all my best wishes, but I've got to get back to work."

"Okay."

"See you later. Good luck."

"Thanks. I could use a little."

And within a matter of hours, I got some. Though maybe it's not called luck when, as you look around, you no longer fail to recognize the obvious.

I spent the rest of the afternoon in the guest room, where I'd locked Rutka's files, rummaging through them trying to make some simple key I'd somehow missed before jump out at me. None jumped.

At five, with my headache back, and feeling sicker than ever of the whole thing, I went back down to the kitchen and faced what I realized was the other cause of my headache, which was a sickness of the heart. I opened the Fed-Ex package from New York. The hypodermic and the vial accompanying it had been well insulated for shipping and had arrived intact along with a typewritten set of instructions that were so clear they appeared to be impossible not to follow. Loving care had gone into their composition. No personal note was enclosed in the package, just the hypodermic, the vial, and the well-written instructions.

I stuffed the instrument and the vial with its harmless-looking cloudy fluid into a flight bag along with the typed instructions for what felt to me exactly like murder, and I drove with a pounding heart over to Albany Med. I was Raskolnikov, General Schwarzkopf, Albert

Schweitzer, Leopold and Loeb, Mother Teresa, Charles Manson.

"Hi, how's he doing?" I said, standing next to the curtain with the skeletal Hispanic man behind it.

Mike said nothing, just stared at the bag that hung from my shoulder.

Mrs. Meserole said, "There's no change, Donald. All we can do is pray. It was good of you to come."

I wondered if there was some way I could stick the lethal needle into her, but this was not what Mike had in mind, or what Stu would have wanted—so far as I knew—so I acceded to the wishes of others in choosing who in the room would be eased over the precipice.

"I'm sorry," I said.

"Yes, it's so sad. But he's so peaceful."

Mike followed me into the corridor. I handed him the bag. "There are clear instructions inside," I said.

He placed the strap over his shoulder and caressed the bag, as if examining its strange properties with his fingertips.

"She's leaving at six," Mike said, "to go with her sister to the movies. It seems I've finally earned her trust."

"Oh."

He shrugged miserably.

"You don't have to do it now," I said. "Or at all. He's not suffering."

"I'm not doing it for him," he said. "I'm doing it for me. I want this over with."

"Sure."

"Maybe I'm doing it for Rhoda and Al too, because it's what they want, but they don't know it. Is that too presumptuous?"

"I think it is."

He thought about it. "Yeah, but—I can't live this way. Maybe they can, but I can't. Don't I count?"

"Yes. What you're doing's not wrong. He's as good as

188

dead, after all. Stu's long gone. What's going on now is just ceremony."

"Well, it's the longest damn ceremony I've ever had anything to do with."

This was where Stu was supposed to stick his head around the corner and say, "Didn't you watch the Academy Awards this year?" But he didn't do it.

I said, "I'd do it for you, but I don't think you want me to. It's too— It's about as intimate as two people can get."

"That's right, Don," he said. "That's exactly what it is. Thanks for your help." He pulled my cheek against his and held it there, and then he turned with the bag on his shoulder and walked back into the room.

I stood there for a minute, feeling light-headed, and wondering if there was a lounge nearby where I could sit down for a while, or maybe curl up in fetal position and weep, when two people walked out of the room across the hall where the comatose truck driver and Bishop McFee lay.

One of the two was a middle-aged woman with a tight perm in a primary color. She said, "Arthur's been a tower of strength through all of this, Edna, so I don't think it's up to you to criticize him."

"June," said the other woman, equally permed to within an inch of her life, "he had no right to talk to you that way about your own brother. I'm sure the Murphys have a skeleton or two in their own closet somewhere, and Arthur just had no right."

"Mrs. Murphy," I said, and she turned. "I'm so sorry about your brother. Has he shown any signs of improvement?"

"No," she said, and both women gazed at me mournfully. "The bishop is sleeping peacefully, but we don't know if he's going to wake up or not."

"It doesn't look good," the other woman said.

189

June Murphy said, "All we can do is pray. We just hope the bishop is having sweet dreams."

"It's a tragedy," I said. "How long has he been in his coma?"

"Since June eleventh. It's coming up on seven weeks now. We're all praying for a miracle."

"But it doesn't look good," the other woman said.

"Your brother—what? Slipped in the rectory?"

"One of the brothers had just waxed the floor," June Murphy said somberly. "Mort was hurrying down the hall and he slipped and fell backwards, and he tragically landed on the back of his head and it affected his brain. And he'd been so vigorous and active right up until the time of the accident."

"And so admired throughout the diocese," I said. "I'm Bob Mills, by the way, and I know your husband, Art. We've bowled together." They both nodded and smiled wanly. "Sometimes I gave your husband a lift on Wednesday night when your brother was using his car."

It took a second for this to register, but then it did, and she said, "Oh, yes, the bishop always left his car to be waxed out at Byrne's Wednesday night and Mortimer used Art's car to make his calls. Wednesday night was his night to visit the homeless. Mortimer never forgot the unfortunate, even after he became a media personality."

"I suppose the bishop's accident must have been almost as hard on Art as it was on you, Mrs. Murphy."

I could see that this made them both a little uncomfortable, and she said, "Yes, Arthur is deeply saddened," and let it go at that.

"Maybe I'll just look in on the bishop and say a little novena," I said.

"Thank you," Mrs. Murphy said. "It's all anyone can do now."

We said good-bye, and as the two moved on down the

corridor I heard Mrs. Murphy's friend say, "Well, now, that was nice of him, wasn't it?"

I walked into the room past the vacant-eyed truck driver and stood at the side of the bed of the vacant-eyed bishop. He was surrounded by flowers and cards and statuary, as if he'd already arrived at the cemetery, but instead of a white clerical collar around his neck, he was hooked up to a feeder and a respirator, and he had a big white bandage wrapped all around his head.

I leaned down to his ear and whispered, "Hello there, All-American Asshole Mega-Hypocrite."

If, in his mind, he formulated a furious reply, he did not speak it.

23

I drove over to the *Cityscape* office on Greene Street and found Joel McClurg about to leave for the day.

"Do you keep a *Times Union* library?"

"Only as far back as '76."

"Good enough."

"What are you looking for?"

"I found John Rutka's Mega-Hypocrite—the one he told you was evil and John was scared to death of. Now I want to find out how he knew the man was evil. I'll bet I know, but I want to confirm it."

McClurg's eyes got big. "You actually found the guy that killed Rutka?"

"No, not yet. That's somebody else. That part will be simple, I think. But first things first."

"You're not telling me a thing, Strachey. And after all the help I gave you."

"Just let me look something up. Then we'll take a ride and you can take a picture of the murder car. How would that be? Or do you have someplace else you have to be?"

McClurg led me quickly to the *Times Union* index and

showed me how to use it. Within a minute I'd found the October 1982 newspaper with the front-page story on Father Mortimer McFee's investiture as bishop of the Albany diocese. The ceremonies were of only passing interest to me; it was Father McFee's background I wanted to learn about, and I did.

Born in Buffalo in 1931, and raised there, Mortimer McFee had attended seminary in Batavia and served as assistant pastor at a church in New Rochelle for three years. Then he became pastor at St. Joseph's in Watertown, where he ministered from 1956 to 1968. In April of 1968 Father McFee was appointed parish priest at St. Michael's in Handbag, where he served until his elevation to bishop of the diocese in 1982. During Rutka's troubled teen years, full of turmoil and lies, his parish priest had been Mortimer McFee.

As we drove out to the diocese headquarters in Latham, I described to McClurg the chain of evidence and happenstance that had led me to Bishop McFee—from the All-American Mega-Hypocrite listed in Rutka's index but missing from his files, to Nathan Zenck, to Bruno Slinger, to Ronnie Linkletter, to Jay Gladu, to Royce McClosky, to Art Murphy, to June Murphy, to the room at Albany Med I'd stood across from nearly every night for a month.

McClurg took notes and gasped quite a bit. He shouldn't have been shocked. It was the oldest story in human history—not that a new bunch of pious phonies didn't keep showing up every generation to imbue the story with a grand new stench.

McClurg said, "When this comes out, aren't you afraid Ronnie Linkletter will kill himself?"

"I don't think so. I think Channel Eight will release him from his contract and he'll get a job in Gum Stump, Idaho, where he'll boost the ratings of whoever hires him. Ronnie's sweet-looking, he opens his mouth and mind-numbing inanities fall out, and he can tell when it might rain. Ronnie wants to be on television more than he wants to die, and a man like that has a future in American broadcasting."

"But if you're right about who killed Rutka, Linkletter will have to testify at the trial. He was there the night the mirror fell and the white Chrysler showed up."

"I feel bad for Ronnie," I said. "But he knew the character of the man he lay down with, and he's paying the price. Causes have effects. Acts have consequences. If Linkletter had come out and come to terms with his homosexuality and grown up, none of this would have happened to him."

McClurg shuddered theatrically. "Jesus, Strachey, you sound just like John Rutka—really quite pompous. I'm not gay, but I'll bet it's not as easy as that. Straight people hardly ever change their personalities and just start being sensible all the time and unaffected by the past. Are gay people superhuman that they should do any better?"

There was a logic to what McClurg said, which I immediately recognized because it was in many ways my own. But there was more to it, too.

"Up to a point," I said, "I agree with you. But when somebody's fear and self-loathing and self-delusion can actually get somebody killed, then we have to say: He should have done better. None of the people in the McFee-Linkletter-Slinger axis behaved as well as he should have—had to have done—and John Rutka lost his life as a result. And my guess is, during his adolescence Rutka lost something else to the demented Mortimer McFee, and that's what set all this violent craziness in motion."

"We'll never know for sure."

"No," I said, "but with Rutka dead and the bishop as

good as dead, it's all academic now. Except, of course, for the killer of John Rutka."

At a quarter of seven we drove into the stone-walled grounds of the beaux-arts mansion that housed the diocese administration offices and the living quarters for Bishop McFee and his staff. The beds of purple snapdragons blooming on either side of the main entrance were lovely next to the shiny car under the porte cochere, a big white Chrysler.

No one appeared to greet us as I parked behind the Chrysler, and no one came out to inquire when I removed from my wallet the photocopy Bub Bailey had given me, of the slice of mud flap found outside the Rutka house after the murder. I crouched down, found the mud flap on the Chrysler that had a slice missing—it was the rear left—and held the photocopy up to it. The fit was perfect. I had found the murder car. McClurg took notes and pictures.

Still, no one appeared—we were not expected, after all—so we got back into my car and drove over to Route 9. I phoned Bub Bailey from the diner where McClurg and I had a couple of burgers, and Bailey agreed to meet us outside the eatery at eight. I phoned Timmy, who wasn't home and was probably at Albany Med, I guessed, and left the message that it was nearly all over and I'd see him later at home.

Bailey showed up promptly at eight with a Handbag patrolman and two state police detectives. I gave them a six-minute version of what I had learned and approximately how I had learned it, leaving out the blackmail, Dirty Harry tactics, impersonating an FBI agent, etc. They listened very, very gravely. The two detectives then took Bub Bailey aside and they conversed quietly. They knew they would have to either act or kill both Joel McClurg and me. Bailey must have advised acting—or maybe the state cops were professionals, too—because that's what we did next.

I followed the two police cars to the diocesan mansion. Bailey matched up the murder-scene mud-flap slice, which he had brought along, with the incomplete flap on the Chrysler. Then we followed him up the steps and pushed a button. Something went ding-dong deep inside.

The priest who came to the door looked downcast at the sight of two police cars, but he ushered us inside, where we gathered in a sparsely decorated lobby with highly polished marble floors but little else in the way of furnishings. He identified himself as Father Andrew Morgan and said he was the bishop's secretary and what was the problem?

When Bailey introduced all of us, the two state troopers said wait a minute, no press, so McClurg was sent outside. I could see him peering through an open window and snapping pictures of us during the exchange that came next.

"Father, we're investigating the murder of a man by the name of John Rutka," Bailey said. "Maybe you've heard about it."

"The homosexual activist?" His rosy cheeks got redder.

"That's right. That's the man. Would you tell me, please, who is the owner of that car in the driveway, the white Chrysler?"

"Why, it's the diocese car. It's owned by the diocese."

"Who drives it normally?"

"The bishop does. He did until his accident. Or I do."

"Who was driving the car last Wednesday night? The bishop was in the hospital, of course."

He pursed his lips and furrowed his brow. "Wednesday, Wednesday."

"Wednesday, two nights ago."

"I think I may have been out doing some shopping

Wednesday night. Yes, I believe I visited Bishop McFee in the hospital and then I ran some personal errands."

"Father, I have to tell you that I've got physical evidence connecting your car with the house in Handbag that John Rutka was abducted from Wednesday night and then murdered and his body burned in an arson fire. Could we go somewhere and talk about this? And I'm required to tell you that you may want to have an attorney present if you wish."

One of the troopers said, "That might be a good idea, Father."

This was taking too long. I said, "Fountain of Eden Motel. On June fourteenth you and another priest drove the Chrysler out to the Fountain of Eden Motel on Central Avenue after you'd taped over the license plates, and you rescued Bishop McFee—who'd been clobbered by a falling ceiling mirror while he was fucking the Channel Eight weatherman—and you brought him into Albany Med and told them he'd slipped on the freshly waxed floor. How did you explain the cuts? Did you say he was carrying a vase of holy water when he tripped, or what?"

Father Morgan took one step backward, then another. Then he just sat right down on the shiny floor as if his legs had turned to water, and he looked up at us and began to hyperventilate.

Later, back at the house, Timmy said, "Before you tell me anything, I have some news. Two things happened at the hospital tonight."

"What?" I knew what one was.

"Stu died." Tears rolled down his face. "And Mike said to tell you that he didn't need the stuff. I know what that means, but anyway he said he didn't need it. He wanted you to know. Stu just let go, Mike said—died on his own."

"The poor guy."

"Yeah."

"How's Mike?"

"Fine."

"How's Rhoda?"

"She wasn't there. I don't know."

"Oh."

He said, "Did you hear what else happened?"

"No. Did the bishop die too?"

"Unh-unh. It was the miracle so many had been praying for."

"Oh, no."

"The bishop woke up. He just blinked awake while the mayor and his wife were in the room praying over him, and the old guy looked around and asked what all the flowers were for. Pretty nifty, huh? Now tell me about your evening."

24

The story was too late for the *Times Union*'s
deadline, but Joel McClurg called in his staff at eleven
Friday night and paid his printer a cash bonus out of his
own pocket, and on Saturday morning the weekly *Cityscape* put out the first extra in its history.

Father Morgan was to have been arraigned at nine A.M.,
but all the Albany judges recused themselves and plans
were made for a late-afternoon hearing to be presided
over by a Presbyterian judge driving in from Erie County.
A diocesan attorney would say only that Father Morgan
would plead not guilty to the murder charge. The lawyer
refused to comment on "related allegations," meaning
the report in *Cityscape* of "antigay Bishop Mortimer
McFee's history of homosexual assignations that were
brought to light by Handbag police and by Albany private investigator Donald Strachey in the John Rutka murder investigation."

By nine Saturday morning, the comatose truck driver
had been moved across the hall to the bed occupied until
the night before by Stu Meserole, and the bishop's room

had a police guard and a diocesan PR flack by the door.

"The outrageous statements about the bishop that were published in a radical publication may be actionable," the PR man told the fifteen or twenty reporters who showed up, but he said he wasn't going to "dignify the report by getting into specifics."

The funeral mass for John Rutka at St. Michael's in Handbag was now news, too. The local mainstream print reporters and the TV knuckleheads were there in force, racing to catch up with *Cityscape*. I also recognized in rear pews the Albany bureau chiefs of *The New York Times, Newsday,* and a free-lancer I knew who had been trying for years to sell something to the *National Enquirer*. He was beaming.

I arrived with Timmy and referred all questions by reporters to Bub Bailey, who in turn advised the press to attend the arraignment that afternoon for a full reading of the charges and a presentation of evidence.

Bub pulled me aside and said, "Thanks for your help."

"Always glad to lend a hand to a professional."

"I've wanted to nail him for years."

"Father Morgan? He's killed other people too? What do you mean?"

"Nah, the bishop. When he was in Handbag, he always had a boyfriend—usually underage. Three fathers came to me over the years he was in Handbag and said McFee was molesting their sons, but when I'd talk to the boys, they'd refuse to cooperate. McFee was shrewd. He'd spot the ones who were gay—whether they knew it yet or not—and he'd—what do you call it?"

"Bring them out."

"This one kid absolutely refused to press charges, but he told me the whole thing. McFee convinced him he was rotten and sinful and corrupt, and then McFee took advantage. The kid believed he was rotten and corrupt, because he knew by then where his sexual interests were and McFee knew too and had him in his power. It must have been hell for those boys. He's an evil man, and he's no Christian, and the humiliation being heaped on him now is what he's had coming for a long, long time."

I looked Bailey hard in the eye. "You knew before I did that McFee was mixed up in this?"

"Nope. How could I? I didn't have John Rutka's famous files to help me in my investigation. They're in Utica, remember?"

His expression didn't change at all. "But you knew where to look even without the files, and who to talk to. I guess you're smarter than I am."

I said nothing.

"It's just a shame John Rutka isn't alive to see justice done," Bailey said. "I'm reasonably certain he was one of McFee's adolescent victims and that's what drove young John to expose exploiters and phonies. I wonder why he didn't out McFee sooner? If he had the goods on Ronnie Linkletter, he must have had the same goods on McFee."

"Who'd have believed him?" I said. "Linkletter and all the people at the motel would have denied everything. And the bishop was held in such high esteem that the community would have been outraged by the accusation, and Rutka might just have had some awful accident, or he'd have been pounded senseless by a couple of Albany police detectives who claimed he resisted arrest in a drug deal. Even though McFee may have been the man he most wanted to get, that's one outing Rutka couldn't have gotten away with."

"I suppose you're right."

"It's only with the pressure of the murder investigation," I said, "that all the principals are being forced to tell what they know and the bishop is being revealed as a mega-hypocrite. Without the murder investigation, it could never have happened."

"It's a cruel irony," Bailey said, shaking his head. "It's a good thing, too, that you happened along to solve the case. I doubt I could have done it on my own—me not being nearly as smart as you are, Mr. Strachey."

"Give me a break," I said. "Okay, so I've got the files. You knew all along I had them, didn't you?"

He laughed.

"Anyway," I said, "I didn't just happen along. John Rutka hired me after he'd been shot in the foot and his house was firebombed. Of course, it turned out he and Sandifer had been behind all that."

"The way it turned out," Bailey said, "it's almost as if he'd planned the whole thing—to expose the evil McFee. Rutka was a devious kid and I wouldn't put anything past him. But I don't suppose he would sacrifice his own life even to get McFee. McFee isn't worth it."

"No, you're right. He isn't."

Inside the church, Ann Rutka was seated in a front pew with her three teenaged children, and behind her were fifteen or twenty people Bub Bailey said were cousins, employees of the hardware store, and the family attorney, David Rizzuto. I sat on the opposite side of the aisle with Timmy and Bailey. Up ahead of us were Eddie Sandifer and five men in Queer Nation T-shirts. Sandifer turned around once and spotted me. He gave me thumbs-up and mouthed what I thought was "Thank you."

The mass, said by the St. Michael's rector, was meditative and serene and accepting of life's vicissitudes, and the Queer Nation crowd sat there and kept quiet. The priest's eulogy made no specific mention of John Rutka's politics or sexual orientation but did refer once to his being a man who "wanted to help the downtrodden."

202

At the conclusion of the service, the coffin was carried out by six of the cousins, Rutka's Queer Nation friends apparently not having been asked to participate.

Outside, I asked Sandifer why he and his friends, who had been so central to Rutka's life, had been so peripheral to the ceremony marking his death.

"He's gone now," Sandifer said unemotionally. "What difference would it make? John told me a long time ago that when his time came he wouldn't mind being buried by his family and laid to rest with his parents. He said himself it would make other people happy, and what difference could it make to him?"

"I'm a little surprised, though, that he didn't insist on a nonchurch send-off," I said. "Knowing what we know now."

"I guess I'm a little surprised too," Sandifer said, and then thanked me for the investigative work I'd done. "I'm going to pay you for your work, too. I've talked to the Rutkas' lawyer, and he'll send you a check when he receives your bill. John was going to pay you and I think he'd want me to do the same. I'm going back to New York. The only reason I came to Albany in the first place was to be with John. But you'll be paid, Strachey."

"If you can afford it, fine. There's no rush, though."

"It won't be long," he said. "Just send the bill to Dave Rizzuto." Sandifer drifted off to the Queer Nation group where they were being animatedly chatted up by Timmy, a nominal Jesuit but actual Platonist who was always ready to let the question lead where it might, short of poor taste.

There was to be no graveside service, just a family brunch at the Rutka house, and I went over to beg off on the family get-together and to wish Ann well in her struggles. Between drags from a Chesterfield, she introduced me to lawyer Dave Rizzuto, who congratulated me on finding the killer and then excused himself and said he had to be on the tennis court in twenty minutes, no offense meant. Ann said she wasn't offended, just envious of anybody who had the time to do anything just for the fun of it.

When Rizzuto was gone, Ann began to thank me profusely for my help, and I said, "I thought after a point I'd be doing it as a public service, but it turned out that won't be necessary. Eddie's going to pay me my usual fee. Of course, he hasn't seen the bill yet."

She laughed. "Oh, he'll be able to handle it. Now that he's rich."

"He is? How did that happen? I thought John just left him a few thousand dollars."

"Dave Rizzuto told me this morning there's a huge life insurance policy with Eddie as the beneficiary. John took it out about a year ago. Dave set it up through his brother's insurance agency, that's how he knows about it. In a week or so, Eddie will be about eight hundred and fifty thousand dollars rich. How's that for not getting left in the lurch? Eddie didn't even know about it until yesterday."

I said, "D.R."

"What's that?"

"John's financial records show fourteen thousand dollars in cash disbursements over the past year to a D.R.— Dave Rizzuto. Why would he have paid in cash, though, and not by check, for a legitimate insurance policy?"

I thought I knew the answer to my own question, but I let Ann, who knew her lawyer, say it. "Hey," she said, "you know how some lawyers are. It was probably Dave's idea. The more untraceable cash they have floating around, the more they can cook the books and not pay taxes on actual income. It was probably part of some complicated scheme of Dave's and his brother's. By

204

going along with it, John probably got a break on the premiums. It's just the way most people do business these days, that's all. It's a lot harder in the hardware business not to be honest, but you know lawyers."

"Well," I said, "eight hundred and fifty thousand dollars doesn't buy what it used to buy, but it's still a decent piece of change."

"Yeah," she said with a raised eyebrow, "especially in Mexico."

"Mexico?"

"Dave says the money is going to be forwarded to a Mexican bank in New York. I didn't say anything to Eddie, because I didn't think this was supposed to be any of my business, and I'm probably not supposed to be telling you. So don't say anything to Eddie. But eight hundred fifty thousand dollars must be about a zillion pesos."

Timmy came over and said, "Eddie says good-bye and thanks again. They're all headed back to New York now."

"He's leaving right away?"

"He's leaving John's car for his niece and he's riding with his friends from New York. They're just stopping at the house to pick up his things."

"Eddie packed up most of his belongings last night," Ann said. "I stopped over and we talked. It meant a lot to both of us, I think. He said such sweet things about John. I cried all over again."

Sandifer and the Queer Nation group were climbing into two cars, one a commodious old Buick station wagon. I excused myself and walked over to Bub Bailey, who was talking with a couple of Rutka cousins.

"Got a minute?"

He followed me back into the shadows of the church entryway.

"Tell me again," I said, "how the pathologist identified John Rutka's body."

"Why? You don't think that's John in the hearse?"

"I guess it must be. Forensic pathologists don't make mistakes, do they?"

"Only very rarely."

"Oh. Only very rarely."

He said, "There was the circumstantial evidence, of course—the wallet, and some traces of clothing. A belt buckle, I think. Then there was the chipped ankle bone from the gunshot wound. The clincher was the dental work. John's records were with Dr. Glossner right here in Handbag and the mouth on that corpse was indisputably Rutka's."

I saw the filthy glass half full of cloudy water on a shelf by the sink in John Rutka's bathroom. I said, "The mouth was John Rutka's, or just the teeth in it? Rutka didn't wear dentures, did he?"

Bailey thought about this. "I don't know. He would have been kind of young. The report just said the pathologist's findings were consistent with the dental records submitted by Dr. Glossner."

I trotted over and caught Ann Rutka as she was climbing into her car. I said quietly, so that her bored- and irritated-looking children could not hear, "Bub Bailey and I are just tying up a couple of loose ends, and we have a peculiar question."

"Go ahead."

"Did your brother wear dentures?"

"Oh, God, yes. Since he was twenty. The dummy practically lived on candy bars, and when he was a kid getting him to brush his teeth was like—pulling teeth. In fact, that's what Dr. Glossner did. John's teeth were so rotten by the time he finished nursing school that Dr. Glossner pulled them all out and gave John dentures. He never seemed to mind, though. By then I guess he had other things on his mind besides what he looked like when he went to bed and got up. Why do you ask?"

"Just something about the pathologist's report. But that clears it up," I said. "One other thing. When John was a nurse at St. Vincent's, what kind of nursing did he do? What unit did he work in? Do you know?"

"For a long time John worked in critical care," she said. "And then later with AIDS patients. Eddie says John was one of the best they had. He knew what he was doing, and he cared. I'm sure it's true. When John believed in something, there was no stopping him."

"It must have been devastating to him when he was fired from the hospital."

"It was hard on him, yes, but I think he never regretted what he was fired for—taking morphine to give to AIDS patients who were in pain. Anyway, John wasn't fired from the hospital. He just wasn't allowed to work as a nurse anymore. He was so well thought of he was kept on in the hospital for several months as some kind of junior administrator until he moved back up to Handbag. Whatever mistakes he made, John was still appreciated."

"What did he do in the hospital after he left nursing?" I asked.

"He worked in the morgue. Creepy, huh? Not for this Rutka, I'll tell ya. In fact, some of John's best friends who came to the funeral worked in the morgue, too." We looked out toward the street in time to see the station wagon and the other car from the city just pulling away. "Well," Ann said, "I've got a house full of cousins to feed, so I'd better hit the road. Stop in the store sometime when you get a chance. And thanks again for all your good work. I don't know this Father Morgan they say killed John, but it doesn't surprise me at all that Bishop McFee had something to do with it. He always seemed to be mad at somebody or something. I guess it was himself."

We said good-bye and I went back over to Bub Bailey. "He wore dentures. He used to work in a morgue in New York. That crew that just pulled out of here, they work in a morgue in New York. They could have filched a male corpse Rutka's size—New York is overflowing with homeless dead people nobody knows or cares about— and chipped the ankle bone and substituted Rutka's dentures for the dead man's dental work. The crude surgery would have been covered up by the effects of the fire.

"Then, all they needed to do to pin the 'murder' on Father Morgan was tear off some of the white Chrysler's mud flap and leave it at the abduction scene. And then make a couple of anonymous, knowing phone calls to you and to me directing us to Slinger, and then to Linkletter, and then onward to the bishop for his grand outing."

"It'd be something John Rutka might dream up."

"That's what I think."

"He was always a boy who kept people on their toes."

25

I told Bailey and Timmy that it was up to me to do what had to be done next. I was the one who had gotten Father Morgan charged with murder and I was the one who had outed the bishop. So the rest of it was up to me too. They agreed.

Bailey said he hoped to hear from me soon. I said I hoped he would, too. He offered Timmy a ride into Albany, and I gassed up the car and drove over to Elmwood Place.

I could see from the bottom of the street that two cars were in the Rutka driveway, in the process of being loaded with suitcases and boxes. I waited around the corner and half an hour later, when the two vehicles passed me, I followed the station wagon, in which Eddie Sandifer rode next to the driver.

We hit the interstate network around Albany, then took the Thruway south. At some point I lost the second car but stuck with the one Sandifer rode in. By one-thirty we were on the Major Deegan heading southeast. I had no food in the car and my headache was back. I offered the toll collector on the Triborough Bridge ten dollars for a candy bar if he had one. He said twenty and I called him a name and drove on. Briefly distracted, I lost the wagon for a panicky quarter of a minute but caught sight of it ahead on the always slow approach to the bridge, which we both crept across. Sandifer's car headed out past LaGuardia, then onto the Van Wyck and finally into JFK.

The late-afternoon near-gridlock hadn't hit the airport yet and we cruised into the lot across from the International Departures complex. I parked and slouched down and watched them unload. The boxes were left in the wagon, but three of Sandifer's bags were pulled out and the two men carried them across the loop roadway and into the Mexicana Airlines departure lobby. After they were inside the building, I followed.

I saw the three of them—Sandifer, his Queer Nation chum, and John Rutka—hugging one another at the end of a long check-in line. Rutka was wearing shades and a tacky blond wig, but there was no mistaking the Byronic profile.

I walked over and said, "Don't you guys ever eat? How about some lunch? Eddie, you're rich, so you can pay."

Sandifer fell backwards, breathing hard, and the Queer Nation man glared and stepped toward me. Rutka just grinned and took off his shades and extended his hand.

I grasped it and said, "Nice work, John. It was your pièce de résistance. An outer's masterpiece."

He looked at me levelly. His wild eye wasn't wandering at all. "I knew you'd appreciate it, Strachey, when you figured it out. Even if I hadn't wanted so badly to get McFee, I still would have enjoyed doing it to earn your appreciation and approval." He grinned contentedly.

"Appreciation, yes, but I have to tell you I don't approve. No, John, I don't approve at all. A Father Andrew

Morgan is scheduled for arraignment an hour from now on a charge of murder. Your murder. You claim to be a man after justice. Is that fair?"

He shrugged. "The guy had it coming. He helped the degenerate McFee cover up his hypocrisy so that McFee could go on contributing to gay oppression with his bigotry and contempt and insane self-hatred. I don't give a shit about Morgan."

"I'm not going to let it happen," I said.

He grinned. "Swell. Good. I don't give a fuck what you do. I outed McFee. That's all I really wanted to do. I accomplished what I stayed in Albany to do. By the way, thanks for your help. You'll be paid, of course. Eddie told you that, didn't he?"

I said, "Eddie wasn't in on it, was he? He didn't know."

He looked less cocky now. "No," he said.

"You set it all up, but you didn't tell him. He actually thought you'd been killed. How could you do that to him?"

Sandifer, calmer now than when I'd walked in on them, but still shaky, said, "It's all right. It was like a miracle. Yeah, I was kind of upset and pissed off for a while. But I got John back and that's all I care about now."

"I hated to do it," Rutka said. "I really did. But Eddie's grief was an important part of what made it look real. After the scams we'd run, it was the only way to go. Maintaining credibility was everything on this one. He understands. I knew he would."

"That's right," Sandifer said. "It was the smartest way to organize it."

I looked at Rutka and said, "How come you've got teeth in your mouth? I thought you left them with the corpse that got burned up."

"I had a new set made first," he said calmly. "Here in

the city. Under another name. The name I'm traveling under that's on my nifty set of fake IDs made up by one of the nation's finest queer counterfeiters. I'm John Gunderson now. Nice, huh? I'll be a Swede for a while and spread socialism in Mexico."

I shook my head and wondered if I was missing something here. "John," I said, "if you fly to Mexico today, you'll really be wasting everybody's time. All the rest of it aside, insurance fraud is considered a serious matter in police and judicial circles. You're going to be extradited and tried and convicted and imprisoned for many, many years."

He looked suddenly somber. "Not if you don't tell them where I am," he said.

The chutzpah. "But why wouldn't I?" I said. "Of *course* I'm going to tell them, you twit! I'll probably phone Bub Bailey from here, in fact, and get him to have the plane held up, and have airport security hold you until the police arrive. Of course I'm going to tell them! Especially after the way you used me, how the hell do you think I'm going to react to this latest of your outrages? Huh?"

He said, "No, you won't. I knew enough about you, Strachey, to be sure that even if you caught up with me this soon, you'd let me go once I told you a couple of things there's no way you could have known up to now."

"What do you mean? What don't I know?"

"My T-cell count. It's about two. All but nonexistent."

"Shit," I said, and looked at the other two. They nodded.

Rutka said grimly, "I probably have a few months, maybe weeks, before I have my first infection. Eddie and I are both HIV-positive, but for some reason his count is normal and he's perfectly healthy, and I'm not. We're giving the money to a clinic some friends of ours started in Mérida where they're developing alternative treat-

212

ments the system here is too slow or too corrupt to let people try. We're going there to stay until we're cured or until we die. Either way, we'll pay our own way and also help a lot of other people the system has given up on."

"By alternative, you mean crackpot, quack—unscientific New Age bullshit. It's a joke."

"A treatment is only a quack treatment if it doesn't work. The forty-two men at the Valladolid Clinic have faith. So do I. So does Eddie."

"Has the system here given up on you? You haven't given it a chance. You're nuts, Rutka. You're wackier than I ever imagined."

"No," he said, "the system here hasn't given up on me. I've given up on it. It's all profits and egos and bureaucrats and politicians and bullshit, and I've had enough of it, that's all. Right now I have the strength to deal with it, but sometime soon I won't. I have to start thinking of myself, protecting myself. So I'm out of here."

We glared at each other, hard. I said, "How do I know this isn't just more of your bullshit—another one of your scams? I've heard all about you in Handbag. You lie as naturally as you eat candy. You're a pathological liar and have been for most of your life. I don't believe a word you say, Rutka."

His eyes were cold now, and he said, "I didn't always lie. I *learned* to lie. Do you know who I learned it from?"

"I know."

"The man is devilish."

"I think you're right about that."

"And I've had him exorcised."

"I saw on TV that it's still done."

"I heard he woke up from his coma," Rutka said.

"Oh, yes."

He was radiant. "Now he'll pay. He's damned."

"I think so."

213

"So let me go. You know you want to, and you know it's right. If you had eight hundred fifty thousand dollars you didn't need, wouldn't you give it to AIDS research and treatment?"

"Actually, I did make a sizeable donation to AIDS care one time when some ill-gotten cash fell my way. But I gave it to Gay Men's Health Crisis, a fine organization whose work is demonstrably excellent. Can you say the same about this Valladolid Clinic?"

"I know the people who set it up and I know they are honest and sincere and they care more about their patients than their own egos. Anyway, since it's my T-cell count that's involved here, and Eddie's in the future, don't you think we should be allowed to choose where our money goes?"

The Mexicana lobby was growing increasingly crowded and I tried to keep my voice low enough not to be overheard but loud enough to be understood by Rutka. I said, "But it is not your money."

"Look," he said, almost serenely, "aren't the insurance companies spending millions of dollars on lawyers and lobbyists trying to weasel out of insuring people with HIV? They'd refuse to insure gay people at all if they could get away with it. They'd fuck us over completely. What I'm doing is not a rip-off, it's just me doing those corporate assholes' job for them. Anyway, what's eight hundred and fifty thousand dollars to an insurance company that spends ten times that much on lobbyists and campaign contributions trying to get the legislature to let the company piss on gay people and abandon us at exactly the time we need the insurance companies the most? You asked me to be fair. Now that's what I'm asking you to be."

I shook my head in wonder.

"Go back and tell them you found evidence that I'm

214

not really dead and get Father Morgan off, but let us go and do this socially useful thing we want to do. Just say you followed Eddie, but you lost him and you don't know what became of him. That's all you have to do. It's that simple."

I said, "How can I be sure you're not making this all up? That it's not part of another devious scam?"

He shrugged and gave me a little crooked smile. "I guess you can't."

Back on Crow Street, I told Timmy, "I lost them. I lost them in the traffic on the Major Deegan."

"No, you didn't," he said. "But I don't want to hear about the con Rutka ran on you this time. And I don't think Bub Bailey does either."

"Good," I said. "I heard it on the car radio. Father Morgan is out?"

"Insufficient evidence. Plus, his hospital-visit-and-shopping alibi for Wednesday night holds up. Lots of people saw him in the bishop's room—I think I might have seen him there myself—and at the Colonie Mall and four or five other places."

"What about McFee? Is he still sentient but incommunicado?"

"He's under guard, but his reputation in the diocese has fallen even further."

"That's an accomplishment. How did he manage that?"

"There was a lot of irrational concern growing around town about how the bishop might have spread AIDS—at church suppers he ate at and so on."

"That's dumb."

"But Ronnie Linkletter heard about it and knew that a lot of people were taking it very seriously and were scared, and he did what he perceived to be his duty as a member of the Hometown Folks news team."

215

"What was that?"

"Ronnie came forward and told a group of reporters that nobody had to worry, because the bishop was always careful and he—he always wore a condom."

I said, "No, he didn't."

And Timmy said, "Yes, he did."

And I knew I was back in Albany.